NIGHTSOUND

TERRORS OF THE SOUL

COLLECTION

JERRY W. MCKINNEY

INTRODUCTION
BY
LORI R. LOPEZ

Do Not fear the Night
It is for Dreams

Nightsound, Terrors of the Soul Collection
By Jerry W. McKinney
First Edition August 2012
© 2012

Edited by
Lori R. Lopez

Cover artwork by
Melissa Stevens
The Illustrated Author

To Ma

TABLE OF CONTENTS

Introduction	**7**
Nightsound	**10**
Feed	**12**
Lie Canthropy	**32**
Paperwork	**46**
In Extremis	**50**
Abe	**61**
Patchouli	**69**
Takers	**81**
Tears of Love	**92**
Tick	**104**
Wind-Borne	**122**
Christmas Spirit	**124**
Flesh & Blood	**133**
Death Bonds	**153**
I.C.U.	**171**

The Fine Print

Ahem. History holds a very long tradition of weaving plots. It is an art as ancient as, well, finger-painting. We all know that it started in the form of oral narrative. Then one day somebody decided to write it down. That's when the real fun began.

There are those who write, and there are those who tell a tale. What you have here is a collection of stories that have been told as well as written with the deft magic and natural honest ease of a born storyteller. You cannot fake this. And those who hear or read such stories cannot forget them. Whether sitting around a campfire or glued to the pages of a book, you are transported to another dimension. You are taken to a level where all that seems real for the moment are the details and words, the images and emotions conveyed by this master who holds you within the story's thrall.

Let's face it, reality can bite. Sometimes we need to flee the confines of its snapping toothen jaws in order to maintain our sanity. Reading these tales might not be the wisest decision in such a case. But if you're the kind of person whose head rattles when you give it a shake; who enjoys being scared to death; who equates shivers of fright with shivers of delight, then feast your eyes on the following pages. You have come to the right place!

Indeed, once you sample for yourself his feverish scratchings, you too will experience the emotional outpouring of awe and fervor that appears to be the typical reaction to this storyteller's art. You will join the growing wave of babbling bobble-headed Jerry fanatics that is spreading around the globe like a zombie plague. Do not take this book lightly, whatever you do. Be aware of what you are getting yourself into: the impatience and distraction; the obsession; the drooling hunger for more horror, but not just any horror . . .

Eventually there will be help. Conniption-Fitness Clinics. Meetings of Jerry Anonymous. For now I can only urge you to think twice if you have not yet been infected. RUN WHILE YOU CAN!!!

Oh, uh . . . hi, Jerry, I was just talking about you . . . Noooooo, I'm not trying to unconvince people to read another of your books. What makes you think that? I was simply explaining how rabid your cult of followers can be! Yes, they are quite enthusiastic, aren't they? Sure, I'll keep it brief. No problem.

(Okay, here are the facts. I was asked by the author to say something here. Preferably nice. But if you want to know the truth, I wonder about this guy. Really! I mean, I really really wonder about this guy!!! Between you and me, I think there's something wrong with him. Something evil. There must be! What kind of mind could write this stuff? He's like some freak of ill-natured —)

Huh? What's that, Jerry? Am I mocking you? Of course not! Me??? Wow. You're just paranoid after the last time. Relax. I've got this under control.

(Are you still here??? I was hoping you would come to your senses! This is not a drill! It isn't a joke!)

Just adding a little humor, Jerry. You know me . . .

(Seriously!!! Take my advice. The guy's nuts! And demented! And probably demonic! Remember his name: Jerry W. McKinney. It's associated with Terror. I kid you not, it's in the dictionary as a definition! So please, whatever you do, DON'T TURN THE PAGE!!!!!!!!!!!!!!)

Lori R. Lopez
Author of *An Ill Wind Blows*

Nightsound

I can hear them moving in the dark. I close my eyes and try to drift away to the point of unconsciousness, the moment of uncaring. Sleep evades me still.

They are in the walls, you see.

My wife would tell me I'm imagining things, that there was nothing moving around in our home except a few ants on the counters and a small spider continuously building webs in the corners of the bathroom.

These are no bugs — they whisper.

Not loud enough to make out what is being said, but voices nonetheless. Muffled sounds of a quiet conversation amid the insulation and wiring of the master-bedroom wall. Every night I would bury my head into my pillow until the pounding of my heartbeat echoed through my skull, the thunderous crashing of blood rushed in my ears. I'd lift my head to escape my body's own noises, breathless, gasping for air. And be greeted with the murmurs of the empty room. The accursed walls.

I need to sleep! God, I need to sleep ...

How could she not hear? I wanted to shake her awake and yell, "ARE YOU DEAF?" But she'd slumber beside me, her breathing mixed with light snores. How I would envy her. Many nights I'd watch the swell of her chest illuminated by the outside streetlamp filtering in through the curtains and count her breaths. A slight gleam would dance upon the folds of her satin nightgown. I embraced these things, the normalcy of life. It kept my mind off the sounds ...

Until the scratching began.

I had to concentrate to hear it at first. No more than a modest scraping on the backside of the wallboard. I sat up at the edge of the bed and listened. My ears have become fine-tuned to even the smallest sound. It was growing. Standing up, I silently crossed the throw rug on the hardwood floor. A misplaced step had my toe bump the molding and the scratching stopped. I held my breath with my ear turned to the wall. Not a single sound did I make. My wife's breathing seemed so loud from the bed. She turned on her side and the sheets played a symphony of notes sliding across her skin. Issuing a moan, she cleared her throat before falling back into the dream world..

As if they could no longer control themselves, the things on the other side of the wall giggled with glee. My heart hammered in my chest and I stumbled backwards. My jaw dropped open. I ran to flick on the light and looked out the bedroom door to the other side of the wall. There was nothing there, yet the laughter continued.

I beat on the accursed spot with my fists, yelling out, "Shut up! Damn you, be quiet! Leave me alone!"

"Alone?" something chortled with a deep gravelly tone. "There's always room for more." After a hideous round of laughter, it was silent once again. I closed my eyes and screamed, then felt claws grip my arm and putrid breath on my face. I stared into the face of madness. "Welcome," the spirit bade. Paralyzed in fear as it pulled me closer to its gaping maw, I fell into the darkness.

We talk among ourselves to pass the time. I know you are awake. I can hear you.

We're in your wall, you see.

Feed

"I'm sorry." Penny peeked at me through the drape of black hair covering her down-turned face. Using the heel of her hand, she wiped a smear of crimson across her lips — my blood. The bitch just bit me. It was a reflexive move; my arm had sent her sprawling when I felt the pain. I looked across the bed with my hand holding my shoulder. The blood escaped between the grip, running small rivulets down my chest. Her eyes were not upon mine but my wound. Sensing she wanted more, I backed to the wall, in shock and unsure of my next move. Penny crept slowly towards me, making guttural sounds as she neared.

For weeks I had been watching her in the bar. Penny's dark hair, contrasted by near porcelain skin ... I was completely entranced. Her subtle moves and stares had always been directed toward others, until tonight. She didn't wait for me to ask but took my hand as we walked into the night. Totally enthralled by the wondrous ecstasy that was to come in her arms, the moments of pure pleasure that seemed inevitable as she led me to her bed — nothing could be more perfect. As we disrobed, her cold touch caressed a multitude of shivers through my body. I closed my eyes as Penny embraced me tightly, and then sank her teeth into my shoulder.

She crawled across the bed, cutting me from escape. In a sudden motion, the dark-haired beauty turned to pounce.

"Mommy?"

The boy looked younger than five years old. His

hand still perched on the doorknob as he looked into the gloom at Penny.

"Mommy, I'm hungry. It hurts, Mommy."

"Oh Max," she comforted while wrapping her nakedness in a sheet. "Let's get you taken care of." Penny returned her attention to me. "Please don't leave, we have to talk."

I nodded to her, but had no intention of hanging around. I didn't want anything to do with this kinky shit. Slipping on my pants as she led the boy through the door, gathering my things quickly as possible, I looked out into the main room in search of an exit. Penny withdrew a cat from a cage. The feline twisted and hissed as she snapped its neck. The boy stared up with eager eyes and tore into it with a ravenous zeal.

Heck, I didn't leave ... I ran.

Morning came and went. I spent the daylight hours huddled behind the room-darkening shades that covered the two windows of my apartment. I tried to eat, but it just made me vomit. Knowing that the human mouth is full of germs, I had dressed the wound when I returned last night. The gauze was browning with dried blood, so I removed it. The skin underneath was unblemished. My stomach cramped as the day progressed. And I was quite surprised by a knock on the door as the sun fell past the horizon. I opened the door slightly until seeing who it was, then pushed it back.

"Ian? I just want to talk, please let me in, it's important." Her voice seemed sincere. "Are you sick, Ian? I can help. I promise."

My stomach took that moment to double up in an extremely painful knot. I fell to my knees. Hearing me cry out, she pushed on the door. The frame splintered as if it were balsa wood. With unbelievable speed, she held my head in her arms. Using a fingernail to dig a scratch on her forearm, Penny pressed it to my lips. It was cold and sweet, yet it burned in my mouth. The suffering stopped immediately. The ecstasy! My mind became aware of every sound, every movement. I watched her chest heave in a long sigh and her eyes roll back. No orgasm has been as sweet.

"We need to go," she pled as she pulled her arm from my mouth.

"What? Why? I don't understand."

"Ian, I need you to trust me." Her face was filled with remorse. Those large dark eyes that had haunted me for weeks still held their effect on me. I'd die for her; little did I know ... I had.

The room wasn't cool yet I shivered as I rose to my feet. Penny steadied me before I toppled. Giving me a moment to clear my head, she took my arm and led me back to her basement apartment on the outskirts of the city. We entered and she quickly cast me aside then ran to her son.

"No!" she cried out. "Max, stop!"

His miniature form was huddled over what looked like a teenage girl, teeth tearing at her throat with the same exuberance as the cat. He looked up seemingly startled. The girl's arms still twitched in death throes.

"I'm sorry, Mommy, I was so hungry and she smelled so good."

She scooped him off the body, then cradled him in her lap as she sat on the floor. His chin wiped blood onto Penny's tan shirt. She was staring at the young girl while rocking her son.

"I was so hungry, Mommy."

"Shhhh ... It's alright, Max. Shhhh ..." Continuing her calming sways. "This wasn't supposed to happen." I looked over to Penny and realized she was speaking to me. "Tami Frund is ... was," she corrected herself, "her name. She lived upstairs and used to come down and play with my little one." Penny stroked his hair and kissed the boy. "At least she will never have to feel the pain, the awful hunger of death. What have I done? I'm sorry! What have I done?" As she rocked her child, she looked at me with such pity.

"We have to call the cops. I mean, the poor girl is dead," I assessed.

Penny cried out a laugh that curled the hair on the back of my neck. "Dead? Dead, you say?" She blurted out another hoarse laugh. "We're all dead, you fool. Tami's the lucky one. You were supposed to die. Just dumb luck." Cuddling her son tighter with his head lain upon her chest.

I was speechless. I hadn't noticed until then, the air had a deeper smell. The night had a thousand sounds, all wanting to tell me a story. I heard the legs of a cockroach scurry, then footsteps descending an unseen stairway. They approached and stopped outside the door to the apartment. A hesitant tapping on the door.

"Penny? Penny, are you home? Tami didn't come home. Thought maybe you've seen her."

She placed a finger across her lips to bid me silence. I looked at the dead teen on the floor and my heart truly ached for her parents. After a moment the steps ascended the stair once again.

"Just stay with me tonight and in the morning you'll understand." Her soulful eyes burned into me from across the room. "I didn't mean to bite him. I figured it's not his fault I'm this way. I could raise him as a normal child, no one would know. While playing, he jumped up into my face. We were laughing, and just this once his shoulder scraped my teeth. To another mother, we would have cleaned it well and watched for infection. To him, it was a death warrant. Max has been five for three years now. But I've never let him kill."

A new smell appealed to my senses. I realized it was coming from the body of the young girl. My stomach growled quite audibly. She smelled delicious.

Penny smirked, "You're weak and need nutrition.

But please leave her be, there are cats in the other room."

My mind raced back to the previous night, watching the child devouring assuredly someone's lost pet. Penny didn't move, but cradled her son and they whispered to each other throughout the night. I watched the sun rising from the edges of black paper taped across the window of the door.

"You can't stay here." Standing as she spoke. "Go to the back door and run to the culvert. The shade of the house will protect you. It will be dark enough there to spend the day. They will come looking for Tami."

"What about you?"

"Oh, I need to do something I should have done a long time ago. Now go!"

I made my way to the backside of the apartment and opened the door. The gloominess of the room was replaced by the light outside. It felt incredibly warm on my skin. I began walking to the pipe she had mentioned. In three steps I was running. The air felt like an oven and all I could think about was the cool darkness. I dove into it headfirst. Then turned in time to see Penny, still with her son in her arms, walking out the door. They didn't come toward the culvert, but into the bright sunlight.

I'll always remember those screams.

Bent over, In the early hours of the morning, no one heard the noise or just didn't care. I stayed in the gloom and stink of that pipe all day. Tried to rest, but it was impossible. About midday, I heard new cries of anguish; guess Tami had been discovered. The police drove up quickly in their cars. Drawing back into the black as much as possible, I used the mud from the floor of the pipe to darken my face. The stench was ungodly. An officer actually shined a light in my sanctuary and didn't see me. My senses seemed to be magnified. The light from the end of the pipe was blinding until dusk. I slid out unnoticed in the murkiness of the evening and found my way to my apartment to clean up. Damn, I was hungry.

watching dirt swirling down the drain. The shower water cascading across my back, washing away the traces of that culvert. My mind on my need — the hunger had to be quenched. Dressing quickly, I loaded a backpack with necessities and left. I could never return to my apartment. Too many people had seen me with Penny. They would be looking for me. I had to disappear. The city seemed like the perfect place, already a haven of anonymity for many. Night embraced me.

The pains were coming more severe as I walked to the streets. Bars in full swing, rock music blaring out, and patrons pushing their way through the doors into the city. I had never realized how loud it was or how much it reeked. Alleyways were a plethora of trash and piss odors that didn't help the fact my stomach was in full revolt. A middle-aged woman with tight shorts and a halter top leaned against the building as I approached. I didn't speak a word passing her, just maintained eye contact. She smelled like hell but I was in agony. I stopped at the corner of a building; she stroked my chest with her hand, walking by me. I fell in behind her entering the darkness of the alley. We were not alone. Someone had slipped behind me. I could feel the tip of a gun pressed into my back.

"Don't move," a whiskey-laden breath ordered. Then he fired. It burned with the ferocity of an iron poker. Damn, it hurt like hell. I fell on a grease puddle that had leaked from the corner of a dumpster.

"Oops," the man laughed, and then spat down on me. "Get his shit and let's get out of here."

She knelt and pulled my wallet from my pocket. I looked at her ankle inches from my face as she flipped through my billfold.

"Twenty-three dollars and a library card! This loser wasn't worth the bull..."

And I bit.

Underneath the taste of sweat and dirt, the warm flow of blood filled my mouth. I sucked in deeply. She was screaming as I watched him raise his foot. Uncontrollably, my eyes rolled back while the sweet fluid warmed me to the core. I was smiling when he kicked me unconscious. Then she buried a knife deep into my chest.

The pair threw me behind the dumpster and covered me with trash. I believe they were trying to hide my body; in their own way, they saved me. I watched from under that rubbish as the sun grew long shadows on the wall. Feeding upon rats that came to eat and burrow through the garbage, I began to chuckle to myself. I bet that whore was feeling the pain now, feeling the hunger. As evening descended, I pulled myself out of that alley. Bastards had even stolen my shoes.

I wandered the street that night barefoot and filthy. I never realized how much the city stank. Following a cat into an alley, my stomach was beginning to revolt. A man sat on a milk crate, his eyes watching me as he lifted a bagged bottle to drink. The cat rubbed and twisted through his legs.

"Hey buddy, you look like you've had a tough night." He reached down and lifted the cat to his lap. "You're not hurt, are you?"

I stumbled to the wall as my gut doubled up in torment. With my shoulder sliding on the brickwork, I dropped to my knees. He let the cat go, stood up and walked to my side. With all the force I could muster, I grabbed his legs and pulled him to the ground. He hit hard and as I climbed on top, his fist connected with the side of my head. I rolled into the rubble of a broken wall.

"What the heck's your problem, bud?" His eyes

glazed as the brick bounced off his skull. I dragged myself over him and ripped out his throat with my teeth. The hot blood gushed into my mouth. It was heaven. As I wiped my lips and chin on my shirt, I looked at the life I had just ended ... somebody's son, brother, and maybe even father. I had taken that away, forever. My throat ached as my eyes filled with tears. I had to grow more callous. If my first kill was so tough, I wouldn't last long. Luckily, his shoes fit me.

Vampire? Hmm, I don't know. Where are all the cool powers? The shape-shifting and the super-strength of the movie monsters; was it all bullshit? Oh, but that sun thing was correct. I saw that and felt it. Burns like Hell. I knew I had to find someplace to hide from the daylight. Today I would stay in the city, but I really needed to get to the suburbs, away from the sound and the stink. I broke into a building's basement window.

The room was a myriad of dusty tables and chairs. They were stacked tightly, with the legs stretching out in the dark. An odor of old wood and urine attacked my senses. My eyes had become quite adjusted to the gloom of night; I actually preferred it. The basement was storage for an Italian restaurant whose owner still found value in the age-worn furniture. But the vermin had also staked their claim and scattered as I walked between their homes of forgotten oak and fabric. I made my way to a set of grease-laden stairs and looked up at the doorway. The rats had settled and only darted across the floor but kept their distance. The underside of the steps was a small space, which after evacuating stacks of yellowed menus, would do nicely as a resting place for now. Daylight crept into the window I had entered, but couldn't do anything more than cause a glow in the general vicinity. As I slept, a curious rodent came too close and became a delicious snack. This remained my home for three weeks.

I ventured out a couple times a week and fed upon the homeless. The hunger didn't come every night. Learning from my first exploit, I would smash their heads before feeding; didn't want to play with my food. The concept was almost amusing if not so horrifying. They were like cattle to me. It was simpler to think of them that way. Tried not to look into their eyes; just cattle ... just cattle. By the third week, the streets seemed a little less populated. There were more police patrols. Even in the city it wasn't too smart leaving bodies near where you sleep. I had to get away. The outskirts, the suburbs should do nicely. I could still steal away into the metropolis for my food and go back safely to the ignorance of the outskirts. Finding an abandoned grocery store in a strip-mall was a stroke of luck. The meat department had a walk-in refrigerator that was perfect. I put a mattress in the cool, dark compartment. It was home.

Finding clothes from Goodwill boxes left unattended was a gamble. I had been lucky at times and found things that fit perfectly. I tried to save those pieces for when I went out in search of entertainment; on the nights the hunger did not dictate my actions. I am still only a man.

Her bright red hair fell across perfectly white shoulders, accented with a smattering of freckles. The smile and green eyes she used upon the barroom caught every stare, including mine. With beer in hand, I was perched on the barstool. Not drinking — the alcohol made me retch — I surveyed the room. I had spotted her before leaving different clubs, but this had been the first time I'd ever seen her inside. I left my beer untouched and went into the parking lot and waited. Several times I looked up as the music bounded out the door when someone departed. Leaning on a tree in the shadows, watching the people as they left, I waited. At closing time, she stepped out. I swear she looked right at me in the gloom. Falling back farther into the darkness, keeping my distance, I walked behind her. There was something about this woman; I yearned for her.

She strolled into a canopied cul-de-sac and entered a two-story Victorian home. The branches from the oaks that lined the circle reached out and meshed together into an unyielding barricade against the moonlight. The facade of the house was covered in shadow. A single window broke the dimness as she entered the second-floor room. I scaled the tree in her front yard and sat on the limb closest to her bedroom. A light jazz played, muted slightly by the glass. In my mind she danced, hips swaying to the music as her hands flowed gracefully; but in actuality, she sat brushing her long, beautiful red hair. After the lights went out, I made it back to my sanctuary before daybreak ... and dreamed.

I stalked a young man once. The hunger hadn't been a factor. He was just wearing a long black coat that appealed to me. The evening hours found the library vacant, save for two ladies with the mindset of returning books to their proper places on the shelves. He was intensely studying a passage in the center of a book and scribbling notes. I walked behind him and looked over his shoulder. Several books lay strewn about the table. He had removed his coat and now it was draped over the chair beside him. The notes held multiple lines of scribbles, with "Modern Mythology" in large block letters and underlined twice. I passed by and sat, pretending to read a book, near the restrooms. After almost an hour, he walked into the facilities. I didn't wait, but went to his table and grabbed his coat. A book titled *Vampirism Folklore* was on top of a small stack. I wrapped it into the coat and walked out.

Excerpt from *Vampirism Folklore* by Jason Asters, Goldberg Press, © 1989.

In the late 19th Century, the superstition of vampirism had reached an apex. The European countries that had been so gripped by the fear were cast back into the Dark Ages with a new round of "witch hunts" led by a man name Van Helsing. Soon it was commonplace to open family mausoleums and drive stakes into the remains of ancestors. Feeling that the plague had been eradicated, the turn of the century passed without people needing to hang garlic on their doors and sleeping with crucifixes. As the 20th Century progressed, there came idle chatter of a new epidemic: a less powerful ghoul, still feasting on the blood but more covert due to having only slightly the powers or characteristics of the old idea of vampirism. Small communities were often found vacant in matters of days, leaving families searching for loved ones. It is rumored that the bloodlines are diminishing, leaving the new-age vampire a weak descendant of "The Old Ones".

Rubbing my chin, I read this paragraph and finally understood. I knew I was a vampire, this realization I had come to terms with, but a mere shadow of the legend. The book spoke of a dying breed of the undead, weaker and diminished. Figures, even in death I would draw the short straw. Checking my watch, I noticed that the bars were about to close. Tomorrow I would head into the city again for my buffet of fools, but tonight I had a date with an oak tree in a cul-de-sac. Maybe she really will dance tonight. The jazz played in my head.

I hadn't known that he was watching me until the motorcycle slid to a stop at the edge of my heels. Just arriving in the city, I didn't even have a chance to scope out my main course for the evening. The hunger stayed at bay as long as I fed twice a week, and it was due. He removed his helmet and smiled at me — a nasty, toothy smile. His dark hair was pulled tightly to the back in a short ponytail. A small gold earring of a heart caught the streetlights and gleamed off his lobe. He had truly cold, dead eyes.

"Hey, friend." He accented the words almost sarcastically. "These are my streets, so why don't you be a real pal and quit messing up my business?"

As I started to speak, his eyes burned red. Standing with my mouth agape, it was only seconds before I realized he was gone. Damn, he was fast. I looked down at the key in my hand. The motorcycle stood propped up next to me. Something told me to heed the warning and accept the gift. I drove back home with the wind in my hair. I wasn't looking forward to the hunger, but was truly enjoying this moment.

The loading bay door was slightly ajar. I cautiously entered my sanctuary. She was tied to a pallet, a young street hooker with her mouth gagged. Fraying, thin twine that secured her dug into her wrists as she futilely attempted to scream. A note was pinned through her breast. GOOD BOY. Tears streamed down her face; somebody's daughter. No, cattle. I covered her eyes with my hand and ripped out her throat. I don't play with my food.

Every three days, when I returned from my nightly prowls, I had a gift of some luckless streetwalker or bum. They were always trussed up but still very much alive. It was like an insane room service. If it kept me from having to deal with the stink of the city, that was fine with me. The empty field behind the store held a cache of unmarked graves. Digging them was a small price to pay, but definitely necessary. I could do the work with the sounds of the crickets singing in the night and lightning bugs flashing around me. Gotta love the suburbs.

I tried to stay away but found myself perched up in the tree staring at her through the window a couple times a week. The nights had been cooler and she left her window open. The scent of her perfume played with my senses. Such a beautiful woman to be always alone. I would see her in the bars ignoring the consistent advances of man after man. She'd laugh and dance with them and even spend time at their tables talking. But she'd always leave the clubs alone to sit at her dressing table to brush her hair. Some would say I was obsessed; I'd say I was a dreamer.

I befriended an older man who had the overnight shift at a small convenience store. Often we'd spend hours chatting about the problems of the world. He didn't expect explanations of my life. He had just accepted me. I saw traces of my father in his eyes. Always a kind word when I walked in and he let me use the bathroom to clean up. Howard Jenkins was a respectful man. I often wondered if the bosses had ever watched the security tapes. Had they seen me or just Howard talking to himself in the middle of the night?

I was washing my hair in the sink of the bathroom when I heard the shot. They had taken sixty-seven dollars from the register and the only friend I had. Howard Jenkins was a respectful man.

I held him as he died. Who says ghouls don't cry?

It had been four years since I had been bitten. The memory of Penny looking at me with such pity had faded away. My gifts of food continued three times a week, although I didn't understand it.   Mundane evenings dragged on endlessly.

Getting bored with the small town entertainment, I decided to venture into the city for a change of scenery. All-too-familiar smells attacked my olfactory senses as the motorcycle passed the city limits. A misting rain had wet the streets, which reflected the neon bar signs, leaving roads aglow with reds and blues before my headlight. The muffled music exploded from the doorways. Couples laughed and chatted as they made their way into the clubs. I found a sports pub and perched with my back propped on a wall. The taste of beer floated in the air as I breathed. I bought one but it sat untouched in front of me while I watched the eighth inning of a rather boring baseball game. A pair of young men talked nastily about a couple girls on the other end of the bar. I found myself smiling, enjoying the normalcy of it all. I missed that.

Walking out the door as the bar closed, I found my way to my motorcycle. A large dog lay across the seat. Entrails were ripped out and hanging from its carcass down the sides of my bike. The gore steamed in the night air. It slid off with a grotesque *shlop*. I shivered as I drove back to my home. The dog was laid on the floor when I entered. A sign was stabbed into its side with a fork. YOU FORGOT YOUR DINNER.

I had quickly buried the dog before daylight with mosquitoes buzzing around me. I was never bitten by them anymore; I guess they knew. Yet their drones filled my head louder than ever. I lay that day in the cool darkness, but sleep would not come. Every sound, every smell, treated me to a greater awareness. I could hear the cars driving on the highway four miles away, and smell the rotting bodies underground. It was unpleasant, although bearable for now. I probably could have slept if I didn't have such a pain in my mouth. Biting down on a rag, the pressure seemed to help. I drifted to slumber listening to my heart beating. It had slowed quite a bit in the last week. I felt something was changing.

When I woke that evening, I spit out my canines with the rag. I could feel pointy tips on my gums. Little too old to be losing baby teeth.

Two days later, a restrained hooker appeared on my doorway. I was starving. I had learned my lesson. Her eyes grew wide as I approached, then closed forever.

I had seen it one night waiting in the field in the shadows of the evening. I do not know if my visitor was just watching me feed, but the ghoul was aware that I seen it. Red eyes cut through the dark; perhaps a warning to show me the end of my leash.

Fireworks rained in the sky as the townspeople celebrated their independence. Multitudes of cascading colors were a welcome backdrop as I buried another drained carcass. The distant sounds of firecrackers brought a smile to my face, reminded of my youth. Fleeting memories of family and friends I had thought I had forgotten. Even though I was alone, they were all with me that night.

I had never felt so ... alive. Every breath, every motion as the beautiful redhead danced across the floor, I had to lean over to watch from my limb. Her ruddy hair twirled behind as she gyrated to the music for my personal show. Like fire, it flowed catching the light. She had come home early that night and had almost caught me as I scurried up the old tree. Pausing before she opened her door, I thought I might have been discovered. It was like she was sniffing the air. Odd. Her green eyes flashed, catching the light from the entryway as she entered. The music began before the light came on. I couldn't have left if I wanted to. Damned if she didn't smirk closing the window later. Looking at my watch, I knew I had to rush to make it back before daybreak and ran in the night air, faster than ever before. Made it to my sanctuary in minutes; I was a god.

Dreams came. Beautiful images of daylight and beaches. The paradise of walking into the surf and the water licking my shins. Blue skies with hazy clouds floating by, all so perfect. A life I wanted ... a life. Wiping my brow, I looked up at the sun. The heat coursed over my face. Penny was bent over watching her son building a sand castle. She looked at me and smiled, then looked up and screamed. Fire crept out of her open mouth as her lips blackened and she exploded into a spray of scalding, melting flesh. It covered me as I felt the heat boiling up inside my own body. Screams turned to laughter; my own. A horrific jest that the world had played. I woke laughing still, yet my face was still wet with tears.

That night, I felt my heart slow even more. My skin grew colder and I was without limit. I was tired of being a kept man. I needed to hunt. A hunger burned in my stomach that had to be quenched, tonight. As I stepped out the door, the sound of a man cussing drifted across the field. Not loudly, but to himself. I could see through the darkness a figure standing next to a small sports car. Steam poured from under the open hood. I was next to him in seconds. A salesman-looking type, with perfect hair and a perfect car, was having a really bad day. He never felt me snap his neck. I threw him over my shoulder and carried him back to my place. My newly acquired fangs tore into his neck quite well. I fed for twenty minutes enjoying the fruits of my labors, feeling his blood flow down my throat. Like I said before, I was a god.

Before disposing of the body, I pulled his wallet out. Always could use a few extra bucks. A picture stared at me upon its opening. There was my salesman friend with his mousy brunette wife and two children. As a matter of fact, he had stuffed his wallet full of photos of his family. The children each wore glasses and braces. They were perfectly imperfect, and the most beautiful family I'd ever seen. I collapsed to my knees and wailed out loud. Gods have no right ... I had no right. Mourning, I carried him back to his car. His family needed closure; I owed them that. Leaving his money, I kept a picture. To always remember I'm no god.

Nights continued to drag on as time passed. I tended to stay close and only feed on the street people and derelicts that were brought to me. I found this somewhat acceptable; most were living on the cusp, the throwaways. Most were already thought of as dead by society and probably their families. I felt the power building in my body as my skin grew colder. I was a caged animal held back by the leash of guilt. I studied the picture of the family every night. I knew the freckles that were splashed across the bridge of the boy's nose, glasses pushed up tightly against his face. The girl had the same mousy look as her mother, but her smile was infectious, the glint of her braces catching the flash of the photographer's light. They were happy, the family that I destroyed. They were.

Walking the streets, I found myself looking into the faces of people. I wondered how many were feeling the hunger. It is for more than food; it's also the need to dream. Just as important. You can always die if you choose it. Penny chose it by walking into the sun, in the same way others choose by living mundane lives ... never dreaming ... never reaching ... never feeding their hunger. So many blank faces, tilting back their beers and staring into space. Perched on their barstools as a television drones out the daily sports scores that will not matter to anyone when they're dead. Were they dead already? Never to taste the nectars of life or feel the sun upon their face? I see more clearly now through the eyes of a demon the humanity we all should cherish. Our precious time with each other is often the price we pay for our hunger, our need to ... feed. We are not gods and monsters, but merely men. No one is immortal.

I knew it was time to move on. I didn't know where I was going, but I felt I couldn't stay in front of the unmarked graveyard. I had seen excavation equipment parked in the lot. The old strip-mall was due for demolition and no longer could be my sanctuary, especially if they started digging up the lot behind. I figured, perhaps I could move to farmlands. Maybe the sheep idea wasn't too bad. I could have bet people were a lot more tolerant about a few missing sheep than neighbors. By taking off before midnight, I was sure I could find a nice dark barn or even basement in the pre-dawn hours. But I knew there was one more stop before I left.

Her light was on. I had planned to swing by just to reminisce before straddling the bike again. It seemed luck was on my side and I could steal a final glimpse. As I climbed the tree, a white ribbon with a key dangled from the limb; my limb. An open invitation. I climbed back down. The porch light dimly lit the small set of steps, casting a yellowish glow upon the white door. I tried the knob; it was open. The key had merely been symbolic. It swung silently inward on the hinges.

I had never before noticed how sparsely furnished the downstairs room was decorated. Why would I? The show had been on the second floor. The only light in the room was at the top of the landing where she stood. It passed through her sheer robe, revealing her form in silhouette. Even after the years of watching her dance, I couldn't find the courage to utter a single word. She descended the stairway slowly and gracefully. Her feet seemed to float across the floor until she laid her hand upon my chest. Closing her eyes and inhaling deeply, the edges of her lips turned up as she exhaled a slight moan.

"Yes." She breathed through slightly parted lips. "Perfect." She probed a finger inside my mouth, and then tasted it. "Truly perfect."

I could only stand and watch. There was no tomorrow, only now. It was all that mattered. She took me by the hand and led me to a door below the steps.

"Wait," I managed to stammer, "isn't the bed upstairs?"

She began to laugh. The hand holding mine clamped on tighter than I thought was possible. Her hair faded to white and her skin grayed. The green eyes that shone with the elegance of an emerald turned milky with the millennia of years and began to glow red. A small golden ring gleamed off the ghoul's earlobe. I could see its true form, a hunched-over beast. I pitied the part that used to be human, long gone in the ages of the Old Ones.

"I have a special place for you," the thing hissed. "But first, a little snack." It lifted my hand to its mouth and bit off my thumb. I screamed in pain. It continued chewing as it led me down the stairs to the basement. There were four hooks hanging from the ceiling. One was occupied by a body stabbed through the back. He was missing both legs and an arm.

"Wh-wh-what the hell? What's going on?"

It chortled and crunched loudly on what remained of my thumb. Then it pulled my face close to it. As it spoke, a red spray of spittle mixed with my blood coated my face.

"Humans are too tender and die too quickly. Spoils the meat, you see. Now, a fresh newly mature vampire is a meal that stays delicious for years. I fed you and gave you what you needed. Now that you've completely turned, I will take what is mine."

With little effort, it lifted me onto a hook. I bellowed as the hook pierced my back and held me hanging between my shoulder blades. While the ghoul ripped off my clothes, I watched the photo of the perfect family drift down to the floor below. Even from that distance, I could still count every freckle on the boy's face.

For months it has been feeding on my body. I can't even begin to explain how it feels to be eaten alive when you cannot die. I suppose when it has eaten too much, I will cease to exist. It pours blood down our throats to keep us alive but little else. I don't know when I really died. Perhaps it was the moment Penny bit me, or when Howard passed away in my arms. I think it's when I destroyed the family. I deserve to die; I am a monster.

The lucky soul on the other hook stopped screaming as the ghoul fed a couple weeks ago. I didn't look to see how much was left. I didn't want to know. I don't know if it was proper, but I prayed for him.

It strips the skin away and eats inches at a time. I know I don't have much life left. My limbs have been gone for weeks. I felt my entrails release onto the floor yesterday.

As it feeds, I close my eyes ...

... And I am walking into the surf, the water licking my shins. Blue skies with hazy clouds floating by, all so perfect. The children have taken off their glasses to play and build sand castles. Penny bids them over to help Max dig the moat around his fortress. She stands and comes to my side, wrapping her arms around me. The ebbing tides reclaim the white sands from beneath our feet as we walk down the shoreline. Smiling, she lays her head upon my chest and I tilt my head to the sky. Doesn't the sun feel great on my face?!!

Lie Canthropy

The child ran into town, breath puffing out like a locomotive behind her, passing by people strolling down the sidewalk as they carefully side-stepped the girl with the wild eyes. Tangled hair bounced with each step, her dirty face only cleaned by the tracks of tears. She wore a pink Hello Kitty jacket that was on the verge of being too small, with her hands stuffed into the pockets. One could only speculate what treasures she carried within the depths of its pink lining, as she was always going to the butcher's, always in a hurry, and always alone.

Mack stared out the window of the barber shop as the little girl passed by.

"Ah, see Joe?" He looked back at the barber who was settled in a chair doing his best to ignore Mack. "I told ya, every Wednesday."

Joe Wilkes looked over the top of the sports section of the newspaper, first out the window and then over to Mack.

"I feel your time would be better spent cleaning that dirty window than worrying yourself about her," Joe scolded.

"You know as well as I do we need to find them."

"I think you need to leave well enough alone. We've been living peacefully with them and there's no need in stirring a bunch of shit up now."

"I don't believe you! They've been killing us for years and yet we leave them alone!"

"Aww shit!" Joe dismissed him with a wave of his hand. "No one has been killed in two years! Well, anyone who didn't deserve it hasn't died."

"Tim Clatter?" Mack looked at Joe defiantly. "Tim Clatter didn't deserve to die."

Joe folded the paper up neatly and slid it onto the table in front of a line of empty chairs. A plume of dust flew into the beams of sunlight cascading in the windows.

"Tim Clatter was an old fool who let his anger guide him, or have you forgotten the time I pulled him off of you? With that look in his eyes, he was trying to kill you. So before you start bringing up idiots like Tim Clatter, just remember who you're talking to."

Mack lifted his gaze from the tiled floor until his eyes met Joe's. "He didn't deserve to die that way."

"That little girl had nothing to do with that, so just leave her alone, if ya know what's good for ya. Now do something productive, like taking the trash out or something. I'm tired of paying you to stand around bullshitting with everyone that walks in that door."

Mack looked at Joe as he tried to understand the barber's ... hell, the town's ignorance. Seemingly defeated, he emptied the small trash cans from behind the three chairs into a black plastic bag. He was silent as he completed his task but noisily dropped the cans back on the floor. If it had bothered Joe, he hadn't shown it. As Mack walked out the door with his trash in hand, Joe picked up his newspaper again and sighed.

"Fool," they both muttered in an unknown unison as the door closed.

The girl was aware of all the eyes watching her, all the unwanted attention. Every week she came into town with a handful of dollar bills that were soft with wear. The townspeople always stared as she ran by, mumbling something to each other. Yet when she closed the door to the butcher's behind her, she felt very uneasy of the atmosphere. The burly man behind the counter acknowledged her with a nod and disappeared into the back cooler. Shortly he came out and handed her a white, wrapped package. She unzipped her jacket and slipped it down the front where it felt cold against her stomach.

"Did you bring the extra money this time?" the burly man queried. "I'm not running a charity around here."

Last week when he counted the money she was five dollars short. She knew it was there, but what choice did she have? With a promise to bring the extra money this time, he had let her leave.

"You're lucky I'm serving you at all. You think you can just come in here and act like nothing's the matter, but we know different don't we?"

"It's all there, I counted it three times."

He grabbed the cash off the top of the display case and thumbed through it. She watched with disgust as his lips moved while he tallied the money.

His eyebrow rose as he looked across the counter at her.

"Yeah it's here ... this time," he added with an accusatory glare, but she was already turning away and heading to the door. He just watched her as he stuffed the money into his pocket. He stopped wondering what she was doing with a dozen cow eyes every week. Heck as long as she had the money, he didn't care.

Mack was dragging the trash can to the curb when she stepped out of the butcher's. He noticed how the pink jacket bulged as she began her trek back down the sidewalk. A slight smell of wild flowers wafted under his nose as she passed. Just the thought of her being this close ... all he had to do was reach out and grab her, but that would be foolish. He knew he had to follow her. Mack looked back into the barber shop in time to see Joe closing the bathroom door behind him. Mack was amused that the barber had taken the newspaper into the crapper, like he hadn't read the damn thing four times already today.

Looking around in time to see her turn a couple blocks down the street, he set his bucket besides the building and hurried to the corner. The wind was stronger here blowing the scent of wildflowers away quickly. A fast food bag came blowing down the sidewalk and wrapped around his leg. He kicked it aside and cussed as he noticed it had left a smear of ketchup on his tan pants. Looking up, Mack's heart dropped when he realized she was nowhere to be seen.

"Where the hell have you been?" Joe stood beside his chair as Mack strolled back in.

"Some of the trash blew down the road and I thought I needed to pick it up."

Joe pursed his lips and breathed loudly through his nose. "Doubt that. Oh, never mind. How 'bout getting on that window like I asked you?"

The next few days went on as usual; even Joe had been in a good mood. They passed time between trimming hair by telling dirty jokes and watching Sandra Kent bouncing across the street. Townsfolk said she was just a dumb blonde, but Joe knew better. She purposely gave an extra hitch into her step as she walked by the window, making her breasts bounce in such a way a man just had to look; didn't mean they didn't enjoy every second of it though.

Joe kept Mack busy with odd jobs around the shop even though he could have done them all himself. The elder barber had always had a soft spot in his heart for hard-luck cases and Mack fit the bill nicely. Although they had their differences, Mack was the kind of fellow that was nice to have around. He was always quick-witted and a decent conversationalist. Since Joe's partner had passed away, it was nice to have some company.

"You gonna need help tonight?" Mack questioned just before he bit into a fresh pulled-pork sandwich. Joe looked up from his rib lunch and sucked the sauce from his thumbs.

"Why, did you have plans to be somewhere else?" he scoffed. "The moon is full tonight, you'd better have your ass there."

"Of course I'll be. I was wondering if you needing help setting things up."

"Naw, I've got it. Just be there before nightfall. Once we close those doors they won't open until morning."

"I'm getting tired of hiding away all the time when the answer to our problem walks into town every week. I could follow her and find them, God dammit!"

"No!" bellowed Joe as he leapt up and towered over Mack. "We've been that route. Trust me, leave her alone." He sat back down and grabbed Mack's hands. "Please ..." he was on the verge of tears.

"Don't worry, my friend, I'll be there tonight."

Joe slowly folded the tinfoil back over the ribs and looked somberly at Mack.

"We need to talk, I mean just between us." The barber looked beaten and exhausted. "I know where she is, hell I've always known."

"You've got to be shitting me! Why didn't you tell anyone? God dammit, think of the lives you might have saved!"

"Exactly! Think of the lives I have saved! She's not our enemy, that girl has been our protector."

"What about all the people they've killed? What about them?" Mack was standing over the table glaring at the old man.

"They ... they ... there's no they, it's us and her. That's all. And if you want to look at murderers, just look at the faces on the street every day ... there's your murderers!"

"I don't understand. These are our neighbors and friends, hardly murderers."

Joe sat with an elbow on the table, his chin resting on his thumb.

"That's one of her gifts; she clears our minds of the insanity we all face, except mine. I think it's my punishment for my ..."

Mack sat back down without losing eye contact.

"About twenty five years ago," Joe continued, "people around here started leaving their houses at night and prowling the streets; not all at once, but it spread like a virus. My own wife, Marie, bit my arm when I tried to stop her from going out. You see, she was seven months pregnant. I couldn't allow her to roam the streets at night, totally mindless. She had changed. I'm not talking about sprouting hair and baying at the moon, not yet anyway, but just as wild ... and dangerous. Eighteen people were killed in that first month, all on the night of the full moon. That's when folks really started to change. We found it easier to point our fingers, I mean we couldn't face the fact we were all to blame. Soon, at night, the streets were teeming with growling, snarling people. But you don't remember that do you?"

Mack just stared at Joe with his mouth agape, certain his friend had totally lost his mind.

"Back then I was working here in this same barber shop for Sam Burns. I know you remember him."

Mack could recall Sam, a little pudgy man with veins that spider webbed across his nose.

"There were a few of us hanging around and shooting the bull when one of those fancy sports cars pulled up right outside that door and a fellow dressed in a solid white suit walked in. Pretty average looking fellow, I didn't think much of him just to look at 'im. He ignored me and went right to Sam and whispered in his ear. I don't know what he said, but Sam dropped his scissors right in the lap of Ed Durkins and followed the fellow out to his car. Of course we were all perched at the window to see what was going on. Then the door opened and she stepped out. She was wearing that same damn pink jacket with the cat on it."

"C'mon, Joe!" Mack grabbed him by the arms across the table. "That was twenty-five years ago; you'd better get your story straight before you try to bullshit me. She's just a girl! Not a demon or a savior, and she certainly isn't over twelve. Christ, I think you've been huffing hair tonic."

"Just shut the hell up and listen, Mack!" Joe pulled his arms free and slowly rubbed the dents that the younger man's fingers had made. "She's no damn girl! Now listen, please!"

Mack leaned back and studied Joe with a critical eye.

"Well, that fancy-dressed fellow looked up at the window from where we were all staring and I believe he was counting us. There were six of us all total besides that strange fellow and cute little girl. He seemed content with the audience and placed his hand on her head. She looked up at the man and started swaying to an unheard beat. Her body flowed as beautifully as silk in the breeze. I swear she aged ten years as she turned with her hands flowing in the air. It looked like she was gathering the air around her head with her splayed fingers. Her face was more beautiful each time her hands crossed by her eyes. As she moved, coarse hair sprouted from her face and hands. Her body contorted as it seemed the bones and the muscles inside her were repositioning themselves. It looked extremely painful;

yet, she danced. She threw her head back and gnashed at the afternoon sunlight that gave her teeth a golden color. I couldn't look away, and I knew I wasn't alone. The room was totally silent. Then she bent over and rolled herself into a ball and bellowed loudly before it all stopped. The sound made the hair on my neck and arms stand up as my body shivered. Ol' White Suit reached down and picked her up by the hand; suddenly she was just the same little girl in the pink jacket. She seemed to be weeping. Sam conversed with him for a minute after, and then watched them get in that car and drive away. Then I turned and watched each man who had just seen this performance go back to their chairs like nothing had happened."

"What you're saying isn't making sense! Are you telling me that all this happened and I don't remember any of it?" Mack seemed a bit miffed.

"Sam came in and returned to trimming the few hairs that Ed Durkins still had back then. I asked him what was going on but he just stared at me. I'd seen that stare enough times to know when to be quiet; but that night ... nothing. Marie and I were waiting for the madness to take us, all dressed up for the cold weather while we still had our wits about us. We took off our jackets at ten and went to bed. I held her tight that night, I'm not ashamed to say, I was afraid to let her go.

The next morning Sam had Tim Weathers and Lee Norms in his shop when I arrived. When I walked in the conversation ended abruptly. Sam called me over and asked how my night was. I was so excited to have a normal night, I couldn't contain myself. 'Well that's what we need to talk to you about, and I'm sorry to say you are the only one who can help us.' Then they told me what they needed from me. I swear I died that day." Joe's hands were visibly shaking as he reached for his iced tea.

"So, what they want from you?"

"My unborn child ..." He put his hand to his eyes for a moment. "Our child," he corrected himself. "Seems that fellow had brought what they call an empath into town to solve our problem. All he wanted in return was a newborn baby. Marie was the only pregnant lady around here at the time. All that little girl had to do was dance in front of a small audience every day and our lives would be normal. I told them they were fucking crazy to even think I could give up my child. Hell, I'd just move and let them find some other way. 'Moving didn't work for Irving Severt,' Tim Weathers added, 'guess folks upstate don't care for people walking the streets at night growling and snapping at them. He was found dead two days ago. We knew it would be a tough decision so take this offer home to your wife.'"

"I know you and Marie told em off, didn't you?"

"Two hundred thousand dollars and the keys to the barber shop was the offer. We were struggling financially, God dammit, we needed the money. Marie cried and screamed at me how I could ever even think about it. Had herself so worked up she went into labor right then. I rushed her to the clinic, she cursed at me as I drove. The baby was stillborn. She blamed me. I walked outside to think and mourn alone when that black sports car pulled up; that dark power window went down with a whine. 'We have a deal, Mr. Wilkes?' His white suit looked so clean in the interior of that car. 'The baby is ...' The bastard held up his hand with a sympathetic smirk. 'I know,' he said, 'do we have a deal?'"

Joe was silent for a moment as he stared at the lines on the palms of his hands, then with a low sigh he continued.

"It was a boy ... my son was dead, you know what I mean?" He looked at Mack searching for solace. "There was nothing I could do about that, but I still could secure my financial future and get a normal life back. I didn't say a word; I only nodded at the man. I instantly regretted it. He smiled at me and the son of a bitch's eyes glowed a deep red in the dimness of the car. The window whirred back to life and the car drove away. I watched the taillights disappear until I was suddenly aware that I was not alone. That pretty little girl reached out and grabbed my hand. I swear I felt the weight of the world leave my shoulders. 'I need six,' she spoke in a low raspy voice, 'or it won't work. Every day I need an audience of six for the town to have a quiet night or things will be as they were.' I looked back up in search of the taillights, I had so many questions. She squeezed my hand. 'He won't be back, he got what he needed and so did you.' She spoke with a voice that seemed far beyond her years. I began to ask 'Who is ...?' and she smiled at me; I don't mean a smile of a child but the face of madness."

Joe took a moment, staring past Mack before continuing, "I managed to get five friends together, including you that first night. It is the most amazing sight as she actually transforms into a voluptuous woman then into a snarling wolf, spinning and swaying to the beat of an unheard tune. She danced for us that evening and every night since. She makes sure nobody ever remembers except me. The town has been quiet, with the exception of nights of full moons. I guess on those nights the curse is too strong for even her."

"But that's when the beasts prowl the night." Mack shifted uneasily in his chair. "Right? Or is that a lie?"

"No, that is not a lie, but the beasts are the ones who don't make it to our full moon dances in time. They are our neighbors; we are a town of werewolves."

Mack squinted his eyes in disbelief.

"So how does the full moon dance protect us? Don't we still turn?"

"Sedation, my friend. Everyone enjoys free drinks before the dance; a special punch of my own concoction. I wait until the doors are locked and drink it too, and as the music plays, we drift into unconsciousness: a pack of sleeping wolves. But that's why we lock the doors, to protect ourselves from, ummm ... party crashers. In the morning all you remember is having the time of your life. The girl's dance always gives you that peace of mind, that ... lie."

Joe stood up and looked at his watch. "Three hours until dark-fall. Do you understand why I have to remember? Someone has to protect us when she can't."

"What about her? Don't the beasts seek her out?" Mack looked up, waiting for the answer.

"She's always been alright; stays out by Miller's pond in that old barn with half a roof. Heck, I only see her once a week when she comes into town. She hasn't needed us for an audience for years. I don't know and I don't want to know."

The banner exclaimed: Full Moon Dance. Come party in safety with your friends. Strength in numbers!

Joe looked at the tattered sign he had been putting out for years, making a mental note to have a new one made. The grommet holes had long been ripped out and replaced with duct tape. He smiled and shook hands as the townsfolk arrived. They were happy to come and enjoy an evening with their neighbors. There were always those who didn't make it on time, but the last one that had any trouble had been Tim Clatter. His arms were found the next morning laying in the gutter on Main Street, only to be identified by the large college signet ring he was always so proud to wear. Joe was pretty sure it was purchased at the local pawn shop.

But then there was Mack. He had never been this late before. Actually, he's generally always been one of the first here for years, helping serve the drinks and flashing that infectious smile of his. Joe looked back at Marie.

"I've got to find Mack; if I'm not back in fifteen minutes you lock this door." Marie looked at Joe with a long face, nodding her head in understanding. Joe kissed his wife and looked into her eyes.

He remembered the weeks after their son was born and how she seldom came out of the darkened bedroom. Always with red-rimmed eyes. He remembered the morning she opened the front door and found a bloody carcass propped against the door, it was totally unrecognizable. Joe had disposed of it with the explanation of an injured animal that had crawled on their porch to die. But Joe had seen the blue hospital blanket tossed in the bushes.

Joe had been gone over ten minutes when Mack arrived. Marie rushed to him and hugged him tight as they waited at the door. Joe didn't make it back in time. Mack toasted his friend as the doors were locked, then wept.

The sun poured in between the bars of the window above the refreshment table. The empty punch bowl lay on the floor as a testament to the party that had transpired. The light hurt Mack's eyes as it crept down the wall to where he was sleeping. Marie was already awake searching the auditorium for her husband as the rest of the town slowly arose to make their ways back to their lives. Everyone was smiling and laughing as if they remembered a truly wonderful night. Mack recalled that feeling.

He didn't have it this morning; he remembered everything.

"Have you seen Joe?" Marie's question took Mack by surprise. "We danced and I held him all night. Then this morning he was gone."

"You know Joe," he lied, "he's probably getting some coffee brewing or maybe in search of some donuts."

She smiled and went toward the cafeteria in search of the hopeless.

Taking the key from the nail over the door, Mack unlocked the padlock from the large hasp on the door. A blast of cool morning air filled his lungs as the bright sunlight played warm upon his face. It was certainly a beautiful morning that did nothing to brighten the darkness in Mack's heart. Why this time did he remember everything? Why this time? He knew the answer; he just didn't want to face it.

The barbershop stood noticeably empty. Mack's mood was accented by the line of storm clouds that darkened the afternoon. Marie spent the day waiting at the door of her home, calling all their friends for a chance, for ... hope.

The rain came.

The next day, Mack watched as the girl in the pink jacket entered the butcher's shop. Instead of waiting for her, he turned and walked out of town, towards the answer ... towards Miller's pond.

The aged door boards shook as Mack pushed them over the golden tufts of grass that grew in front of the old barn. The scent of wildflowers was heavy in the air. The barn sat amid a field of a beautiful explosion of color. The blue sky was clear with a single cloud that floated lazily in the sky. Several large birds flew up and then decided he wasn't much of a threat, landed back down and continued their meals. The smell of rot and decay burned Mack's nose as his eyes focused on the six figures propped in chairs, all arranged in a circle. They were all in different stages of decay. Mack recognized Tim Clatter's vest on an armless corpse and realized beasts weren't the only thing roaming the streets of town on full moon nights. Birds pecked strips of browned, weathered skin away from hollow eye sockets.

A black bird cawed loudly as its "meal" shook violently and screamed in pain. Mack's heart jumped when he realized it was Joe.

"Joe! Joe!" Mack called out as he began to cross the barn floor.

"No! Mack! She must not find you here! She'll make you forget! You must remember, for the town, for Marie, for the soul of my son. Please go!" Joe croaked.

Mack slipped into the darkness of a corner of the barn as the girl pushed her way in. He cowered behind a barrel as he peeked out. If she knew he was there she showed no sign but skipped into the center of the macabre audience. Reaching into her jacket, she pulled out the white package. One by one she pushed the cow eyes into the empty eye sockets. Being larger than a human's, the eyes protruded into an almost comical stare. She lifted Joe's chin and using a finger to finish cleaning out what the bird had missed, stuffed an eye into the freshly emptied socket. Noticing the birds hadn't taken his other eye yet; she popped the last cow eye into her mouth and chewed with a ravenous zeal.

With all eyes upon her, she began to dance.

Paperwork

"Yeah, I tell you I found Jake that way," Chet proudly stated over the phone.

Feet on the desk and swinging the chair to and fro, Chet continued: "Mmmm-hmmm, yeah, choked to death and a full-sized stapler sticking right out of his ass. Must've pissed someone off big time."

He reached for his coffee and downed the last few cold drops. His eyes scanned the office until he found what he was looking for. Chet balled up a piece of paper and tossed it across the room – where it struck a thin, sickly-looking man straightening up a desk. Ernst looked over as Chet tapped his empty coffee mug with a pencil.

"Be a pal and get me some coffee, Ernst ... and oh ... cream, no sugar."

Loping over, Ernst grabbed the mug and turned toward the coffee station..

"Yeah, PAL ... Personal Ass Licker," Chet snickered into the phone. Muffled laughter could be heard through the receiver that rested against Chet's ear as he continued swaying in his chair.

 "You should see this guy, thin as a rail, and about as nerdy as they come."

Chet unfolded a paperclip and started bending it into a little wire piece of art. "I don't know, it seems he's been here forever. Doesn't do anything but gopher work. I don't think they pay him much, but he keeps showing up. Must be about fifty and still rides a bicycle to work every day. Not a nice modern bike either. Geez, I think he stole it off of the Flintstones."

Another round of laughter made Chet move the phone a little from his ear.

"The police have been here interviewing everyone for the last week." Chet listened intently as his eyes stared at his fingers bending the little wire.

"No, no, nothing at all. They had me in the back office for at least an hour drilling me." He paused as he listened again. "Yeah, I think it was because I was next in line for his job. Between me and you, I'm glad he's gone 'cause it's a freakin' sweet job."

He jumped a little bit as Ernst set the coffee cup down on his desk. Chet looked up at Ernst and gave him a smug grin. "Thanks, pal." Yet another round of subdued laughter could be heard out of the earpiece as Ernst shuffled away.

"Had everyone in that back room for at least half an hour, except Ernst. He was only in there a couple minutes before he came strolling back out. Jake had been a big guy."

Another pause. "You know the type, went to the gym every day before work, and the smart bastard billed it all to the company, and they paid it! Do you believe that ballsy son of a bitch? Well, the cops figured it took at least two guys to handle ol' Jake. I know I wouldn't have wanted to fuck with him."

Chet looked over at Ernst, who had moved to straightening another desk.

"I've got a few more things I need to look into," Chet said, glancing up at the wall clock, "and damn, it's already almost six." Chet put his feet on the floor as he listened. "Mmmm-hmmm. I'll be there in an hour. Save me a seat. Later, dude."

Hanging up the phone, he looked over at Ernst. "Damn, everybody gone?"

Ernst stopped his paper shuffling and looked over to Chet. "Yes, sir. The place clears out at five mostly."

Up until two days ago, Chet would have been already perched on a bar stool at the sports pub with a cold beer by this time. " How late you stay?"

"About six, sir. That gives me time to clean up. Mother is coming for me, and we're going out to dinner."

"Hey, do you think you could find another place to park your bike? It's kinda embarrassing chained out front like that. It looks like we are hiring the homeless." Chet picked up his cup and took a swig, instantly spewing it back into the cup and getting a few drops onto his shirt. "Son of a bitch!" he howled. "This is a Forzieri, goddammit! Thing cost me about two hundred bucks! It's Italian!"

Ernst came running over with a paper towel. Snatching it from Ernst's hands, Chet demanded, "Gimme that! What the fuck did you put sugar in my coffee for? I told you no sugar. No sugar! Are you fuckin' stupid? You better hope it doesn't stain. I'll make sure it comes out of your check!"

"I'm sorry, sir. I thought you said sugar," Ernst wheezed.

"Just get away from me, please! Why don't you get on your Yabba Dabba Doo bike and get the fuck out of here. We'll discuss if you have a job tomorrow with the higher-ups. Incompetent piece of shit!"

Ernst backed off, his shoulders stooped, and walked away.

Chet went to the water cooler, dampened the paper towel and dabbed the widening coffee spot. Then he decided to leave the stain to a professional. "Old Man Wong should be able to get this out." He chuckled lightly at the thought of Wong saying, "No ticky, no shirty."

Settling back at his desk, Chet reached into the basket on the corner and grabbed the short stack of papers. He began separating them into three piles. "What do we need him around here for anyway?" he mumbled to himself. "Get rid of him and make everybody clean their own stations. Hell, they'll probably show me a little more respect for saving them money."

Picking up a stack, he tapped the edges until they aligned and he paperclipped them together. Likewise with the second stack. As he tapped the third stack, he realized he was out of clips and looked over at the small gallery of wire art he had created over the course of the day. Reaching beside the basket for the stapler, he found it empty.

"Where the hell's the stapler?' Chet muttered.

"Right here," whispered a voice from behind him.

Ernst reached for the phone and called the police. He was distressed to find Chet this way. He would have to call Mom and tell her to cancel their dinner plans. She would be upset. Second time he had to cancel. He had thought he heard her come in earlier, but that was before he had found ... well, it wasn't his fault she was late again.

In Extremis

Mass would be cancelled tonight again for the public.

Sister Claire lifted her head from a silent prayer, carefully crossing her chest for the Trinity. The priest lay tied to his bed straining against his bonds. The frame groaned as he gnashed his teeth, grunting in the endeavor. She had performed his last rites the night before and in good judgment restrained his body. The abbess had seen the dead rise before. She would watch over him and pray for the Father's soul. He was a man of God and she would not defile his body.

With tearful eyes she reached out to his ceremonial robes. They were hanging neatly on a large brass hook protruding from the wall. The wool garment was a deep red with an ornate cloth necklace that lay down the front of the robe. She gripped tightly the cross he had carried so often down the aisle of the sanctuary. The gold glistened in her hands. Claire suddenly felt ashamed as she noticed the greasy smears her fingers had made across its smooth surface. Wiping the cross within the folds of her habit, she felt relief as it cast her reflection back to her in golden miniature. Father Job gasped out a wheeze, fighting against the fabric sashes that Claire had used from his own wardrobe. She eyed her amateurish knots and prayed they would hold. The dead priest hissed.

The sanctuary teemed with the ambling dead. Some actually sat in pews and kneeled in prayer. They wore different states of dress, from a lady in a power suit to a man in his heavily stained boxer shorts. A trail of dried feces caked his leg. The air was putrid with the sickening sweet smell of rotten flesh. Flies laid their maggots on all, without bias. The buzzing became a constant hum in the air. On occasion one of the dead would find its way down the steps to the church rectory, only to be thwarted by a wrought-iron gate that was closed across the narrow hallway. If Claire stayed silent they would lose interest in the empty corridor and lope back up into the main hall. But the flies remained, and buzzed.

Eight weeks ago, Father Job had taken her hand and looked into her eyes. Claire knew what he was going to ask and answered him without a word. The pair closed their eyes and prayed. This house of God would not turn its back on the people of the city when they needed religion; when they needed faith. She had moved a few of her things from her apartment across the street into one of the spare rooms of the rectory. The spiritual needs of the congregation were attended to daily, and the people found refuge in the great hall. When the streets were lighter with the deceased, the Father's own private kitchen fed many as volunteers passed up and down the narrow corridors of the lower levels with pots of any type of food they could scavenge. The volunteers had brought cases of canned meats and vegetables and stocked the small pantry.

Job would preach his sermons with a powerful voice that echoed throughout the church. All would stop and make their way to the sanctuary to hear and hope. Hope ... was all they had left. The undead horde outside would pound upon the barred church doors when Father Job addressed the congregation. It was like they needed to be there. It had made Claire wonder if it was too late for salvation for the dead. As the sermons wound down, all would go back to their conversations and the dead left the church door to wander elsewhere.

She often believed it was a miracle how Job had such power over people. Claire always had such admiration for that fact. Donations were not asked for any longer, but the people were eager to give their time to help in any way possible. Parties were formed to collect food and other necessities. The streets were full of the dead, but they were slow and easily avoided by daylight. Believing in strength in numbers, not weapons.

There were few families left, for the multitude of the survivors had been single folks. No longer could the laughter of children or murmurs of gossip be heard; there was just prayer. The rectory had a shower stall which each person used on rotation. Most scavenged clothes on their raids to change into, yet some tried to wash their clothes in the sinks of the restrooms. The scents of cologne and perfumes hung heavy in the air.

Claire had counted sixty-eight survivors. With her and Job it had been an even seventy at the peak of occupancy. A group of eight went out on a food raid in the third week and never returned. Greener pastures, Claire hoped ... and prayed.

The Father spent his days in his office writing nightly sermons. For an hour of each day, he sat in his confessional listening to a multitude of sins as each tried to cleanse their soul. The charismatic priest always made them feel more at ease. It was his gift. Claire had noticed a few of them actually smiling as they finished receiving absolution.

One young man would sit at the organ every day and play beautiful music, some of which Claire herself had recognized. Most people sat in the pews and watched, sometimes sang. But no one protested. He had played classical pieces with the emotions of a grandmaster and Top 40 with the same exuberance. Even Father Job had sat leaning against a pew with his chin on his thumbs and watched in awe. There were never any thumps or bumps outside the doors while he played. For a short while, everything seemed normal. A young man named Theodore Grimes had brought that back to them for a short time with his music. He had almost become a celebrity in his own way; known to all and embraced as a friend. They missed him. Theodore was one of those that hadn't returned from scavenging.

Once in the night amid the snoring of some and weeping of others, Claire sat in the front pew looking up above the altar. The full moon shone brightly through the stained-glass image of Mary. The light cast a colorful mosaic glow upon her uplifted face. She prayed for her waning strength. She felt someone sit next to her and opened her eyes to a young girl. They hugged each other tightly. Claire had never seen her before, and she knew them all. Feeling the child's embrace dissolving under her grip, Claire smiled and cried as she was left with a small, empty robe ... and strength. She was smiling when Job woke her.

By the fourth week, all but the freshly dead were pretty easy to locate. The odor of their rotten flesh preceded their arrival. Closed up with many people, the church had a smell of its own. It was decided to open the main doors for a short time to freshen the air. A long driveway extended near the entrance, outlined with tall looming oak trees. It was quite picturesque and had been the location of many photo shoots. The sun filtered through the trees, leaving a mottling of light upon a path of small gravel. They had pulled an SUV across the gates to give themselves the false sense of security, but found out that act was useless the first time Father Job began his sermons. The dead weren't noticed until beginning a feast on an older man in the back pew. There had been four of them that time. A man dressed in a red flannel shirt looked up at the first scream. His lips were gone and a string of sinew of the victim dangled from exposed teeth. Claire realized she had known the man in life. The reanimated had killed three before Job ran outside and called to them. Dragging the remains of their victims, the dead followed Job's voice, leaving a large smear of blood across the threshold. Job ran past them, slipping in the gore, and fell skidding on his chest into the vestibule. The doors were closed and barred quickly as the hall filled with weeping. Sister Claire ran to the priest. He was sitting cross-legged staring at the door. The front of his beautiful, white robes were now stained in a deep crimson. He was cradling the cross in his lap. Eyes fixed on the portal; lips moving in a silent prayer. Kneeling beside him, with a hand on his shoulder, Claire bowed her head and hoped.

The dead pounded on the doors. It didn't matter how low Job tried to keep his voice while reading from the Lectionary. Daily the numbers of the undead grew outside the closed entrance. The smell from outside was much more pungent than the stale air indoors. Leaving them open wouldn't help anymore and was basically suicide. The scavenger groups had no problem passing through the few dead that stayed milling around the grounds, using walkie-talkies one group had returned with on a raid through a department store to keep in touch.

The walkie offered only static to the survivors gathered in a circle. They whispered among each other as time passed. There had been no communication from the most recent scavenger crew for the last 45 minutes. After two hours, the radio was turned off. Job gave a somber mass, looking into everyone's eyes from the altar. The organ was silenced forever. A mother knelt down in front of her young son and started a soft rendition of "Happy Birthday to you," crying as her voice wavered. Claire watched as the boy placed his hand on his mother's lips and realized he was deaf. Job looked away and disappeared into the rectory. Claire approached the woman and knelt with her. The newly seven-year-old boy stared at her, his quivering. The nun sang in beautiful acappelia.

Another week passed without incident. There was no more scavenging because the courtyard of the church teemed with zombies. After the last mass, the dead continued beating on the doors for an hour. Job didn't want to take the chance anymore; he quit giving sermons. The survivors huddled into small prayer circles daily, looking to Claire and Job for guidance. The Father was growing more distant every day.

The dead had turned to cannibalism. The ones who had missing limbs were the first to be preyed upon. As time passed, the weather grew warmer and the rotting increased in speed. The flesh on some was blackened and fell off with the slightest jar. One caught the corner of his abdomen on the rail for the church steps, becoming disemboweled. The others rushed to the growing pile of intestines, fighting for their share. He had actually eaten some of it himself before the others tore him apart. Flies were increasingly abundant, laying maggots on the dead. The air was filled with a putrid stench. Yet they kept coming.

Two toilets in the ladies room became totally plugged up and unusable, so the congregation had to share the four remaining commodes in the church. Showers were becoming less frequent. Some would sit in the same clothes day after day. A temporary bout of dysentery plagued the congregation. Mop buckets were used as makeshift toilets and rinsed in a utility sink. Drinking water had all been boiled after that. The seven-year-old wasn't strong enough. Claire and his mother wrapped his body in one of the ornamental drapes that had adorned the walls. The crushed red velour drape was not as soft as the child's cheek. They stashed the bundle into a downstairs closet. Job stayed as the mother was led back upstairs. He struck the child's head with a candlestick, then fell against the wall and ɹilently sobbed. Claire stepped back down the steps and could hear the priest singing "Happy Birthday" under his tears; she left him alone to grieve. The song fell upon deaf ears.

Some of the supplies were running low. Things one took for granted, such as toilet paper and trash bags. The reanimated dead had been quiet for three days. Large wooden doors blocked the view of the steps leading into the church. Several of the men put their ears to the doors, narrowed their eyes and listened. Silence came from both the church and the other side of the door. Whispers filled the entryway; whispers of need.

A group of volunteers was arranged for a small exploration into the courtyard. Each would be armed with a stave from a pew that had been dismantled. The short oak planks made heavy clubs, capable of inflicting fatal damage. Hopefully they wouldn't need them. Claire blessed each man before turning to Job. The priest was standing at the altar looking totally lost. She turned to walk up the aisle of the sanctuary as the men removed the large bar off the door. A beam of sunlight cut the gloomy interior where the men stood with staves in hand.

"No!" bellowed Job. "What are you doing?"

All heads turned to the priest as he looked beyond them to the rapidly filling door of decayed and rotten parishioners who had waited outside the church. Called by the word of God; called by the voice of Job. Taken by surprise, the doors burst in, slamming a woman who was just kissing her husband good luck. The men swung their clubs against the flood of bodies pushing through the doorway. The portal huddled the dead tightly together as they made their way into the house of God. The men failed and were pulled apart by a ravenous feeding frenzy. Job stood unbelieving his eyes at the altar of the church as his home was being invaded by these spawns of Hell. The screams and cries of each man, woman and child burned into his ears and mind. Yet he did nothing.

A wave of fetid air blew across the sanctuary in advance of the undead horde. The survivors were trapped between pews before being dragged down to the floor in a volley of screams and teeth. Claire turned toward the rectory steps in a panic. Job bellowed a cry of anguish; the room went silent. Slowly the dead shuffled to the aisle and in a communion-like line then advanced to the altar. The sound of their shuffling feet drowned out the useless cries for help of the forgotten injured, who lay upon building red stains. Claire was frozen in awe as Job began to speak.

"Per istam sanctan unctionem et suam piissimam misericordiam, indulgeat tibi Dominus quidquid per visum, audtiotum, odorátum, gustum et locutiónem, tactum, gressum deliquisti."

All forward movement stopped.

"Kyrie eléison. Christe eléison. Kyrie eléison. Pater noster ... Et ne nos indúcas in tentatiónem."

They stared up at Job before the altar as he crossed his chest in the sign of the Trinity.

"Amen," the priest concluded, as did Claire. The dead had been given their extreme unction ... their last rites.

Job turned toward Claire and walked down from the altar. The dead did nothing but watch. The nun noticed the priest's white knuckles as he gripped his Bible; she noticed how his legs trembled with each step. Claire backed down the rectory steps with the priest following behind. Her hand guided him, for his eyes were closed and lips moved in silent prayer. As he passed the wrought-iron gate, she pushed it closed. They were not followed.

Job fell with his back against the wall, sliding on legs that could no longer carry the weight. Claire looked down the hall to the gate to assure it was latched securely prior to going into the kitchen to get the priest some water. Job held the Bible to his chest tightly as he sank, his back bouncing lightly on the wall. The closet door at the end of the hall slowly opened, and a small child pulled himself out from folds of fabric. His light brown hair was creased above the right eye. Job's blow had only smashed the ocular orbit frontal bone, leaving the eye a mash of yellowing ooze that dried on the child's cheek. He was merely a couple feet when Job looked up at the boy.

"No!" Job screamed. But his plea reached deaf ears.

The child bit into his arm as he pushed him away. Claire drove a cleaver into the boy's skull.

They cleaned and dressed the injury, each knowing it was fruitless. Assuring each other that they had cleaned the wound well enough, then prayed. Claire had dragged the boy's body to the outside of the gate before closing it again. He had disappeared in the night. She didn't want to think about what had taken him away.

The Father grew sick with fever. Claire read scripture to him and kept cool washcloths on his brow. She took his Bible and read from the Book of James over him. Anointing of the sick it has been called; Job deserved his last rites also.

She fumbled tying the knots to lash him to the bed. Job gave no resistance. His head burned with fever and his lips split open. Claire wet a cloth and he sucked the water from it.

"Please," he whispered in a raspy voice.

She knew why he pleaded but was unable and unwilling to provide, for he was a man of God. He shook violently as he expired. Claire wept out loud until she realized the attention it was causing. The wrought-iron gate was a portrait of rotten faces looking in and groping. She went to her room and cried into her pillow.

The priest snarled and snapped at her when she came near. There was no need to approach him anymore. Claire talked to him every day though. She tried to work things out in her head by speaking aloud; there was no answer. She attempted to stay in her room as much as possible. The air in the rectory was pungent with the sickening stench of decomposition. Claire stuffed towels under her door to filter the smells, also to keep the flies at bay.

Morning came; Claire had only known this fact by the wind-up clock on her nightstand. She quickly kicked the towel away from the door on her trek to purge her swollen bladder. When exiting the bathroom, her knees grew weak as she noticed the gate standing ajar. Eyes darted into the priest's room. The sashes she had used to tie the man lay dangling from the side of the bed. Job was gone. Watching the stairway for the slightest movement, Claire crept toward the gate. The hasp was bent and small pieces of the bolt lay scattered around the floor. It was totally useless. She bit her bottom lip slightly, craning her neck up the stairwell; only silence and gloom. Hands trembling uncontrollably, she pressed them to her side as she slid up on the first step. Slowly and methodically, the nun scaled the access to the sanctuary.

The large wooden church doors stood open, hanging askew. A slight breeze blew through the room. It was the closest thing to fresh air that Claire smelled in days. The room was empty. She dropped her shoulders in relief until a grunt from the left caught her breath. Behind the altar Job stood dressed in his robes, his eyes staring outside with the large golden cross in hand. Claire backed up into the gloom until her back brushed the door of the confessional. A faraway scream grew closer until it was in the courtyard of the church. The nun pulled the door open with both hands slowly and stepped into the small compartment.

A small ornate carved grate gave Claire a clear view as six zombies dragged a screaming woman in front of the altar. The lady was dirty and bleeding and her clothes were torn. The nun noticed the woman was only wearing one shoe. Claire realized if this poor soul was still alive, there had to be others. Job raised the cross high above his head. The dead pushed the lady to the floor in front of the altar. Claire recognized immediately Liturgy of the Eucharist, the collection of alms. With wild eyes, the lady searched for an escape until she looked into the confessional. Claire put her hand to her mouth as the woman reached out to the box. Job brought the cross down on her head, glancing across her scalp. A flap of skin fell down upon her left eye as the woman continued to scream. Her face was a mask of crimson. Job struck again, splitting her skull at the eye socket. The blow sprayed blood across the front of the priest's robes. Her mouth was wide in a scream that wouldn't be heard. Her hand stretched out towards the confessional. The priest gripped her head and pulled the skull apart, the skin stretching wide before ripping. He scooped out a handful of the brains and offered it to each of the dead. Claire closed her eyes. Others started to come to the mass. The room was soon full. The nun gripped her rosary as her lips moved, until she heard the other confessional door open.

Job had come to hear her sins.

No hope, only prayer.

Amen.

Abe

Abe opened his eyes. He felt her breath on his back and smiled in the comfort that she was still there. He woke several times in the night to reach back and feel her form, her heat, resting against his skin. He was sure madness would follow if she was gone, as it had happened before. Abe closed his eyes. He didn't want to think about those times, he just wanted to concentrate on her steady breathing. It gave him goose bumps. He sat up on the edge of the bed and looked down at her mascara-filthy eyes, smearing dark stains on his clean pillow cases. Irritated by this, he grabbed the bonds that held her hands and snatched her up. Abe didn't want this one messing his sheets too. They always did. Bitches.

It always amazed Abe how quickly a woman followed directions. A threatening look and a forceful tug on her bonds and she was a lamb. She stood before him with wide red eyes, a ghost of the playful flirtatious eyes that stared at him at the bar last night. She learned fast, but not without testing her limits; a fresh set of bruises around her arms could attest to this fact. Not the face; never the face. He untied her hands and led her to the bathroom. He liked this one a lot, she was quiet. The last one, a fiery redhead, screamed like mad. Abe finally super-glued her lips together to stop her persistent howling. She had screamed horribly when she finally ripped her lips apart ... well, almost apart. The top lip had stayed attached to the lower, just torn above. It was almost comical watching her scream out from above her two closed lips, but he threw her down and stepped on her neck to shut her up. She hadn't lasted long.

He sat outside the door while the current woman showered, always mindful of the time limit he set to clean herself. He never watched them shower; he didn't want to be considered a pervert. Abe was a gentleman, a damn fine catch, according to his Aunt Diane. She should know. After his parents died in a car crash, his relatives took him in. He was sixteen then and it was a seemingly loving household. Abe had been content to finish school and live with his easily controlled aunt and uncle. A couple of years passed and living there was better than fending for himself. Free room and board, then came the perks. Very often after hearing his uncle begin his nightly snoring did his aunt visit his bed. At first Abe felt wrong about it but surmised that she wasn't blood-related and being eighteen he had urges, needs she was willing to fulfill. Abe had grown quite accustomed to this arrangement, yet he felt so empty as he watched his aunt leave his bed with his semen running down her thighs.

One morning Abe woke to his Uncle James standing over him, spurting a stream of obscenities. His face was a mask of ugly red with slotted eyes, and he spit a steady spray as he yelled. Abe stared, not hearing the nasty words but the smacking sounds his wet lips made as they slapped together, and couldn't help but pity this waste of life. Looking up at the man, noting his uncle was clad in a pair of red satin pajamas, his stomach turned.

"You need to be a man," Abe sneered as he sprang from bed and hit him under the jaw with his fist. Uncle James reeled back, his mouth emitting a spray of blood and spit while he hit the wall. Looking down into his uncle's fearful eyes, Abe pulled his penis out of his boxers and urinated on the man. As Abe left their house, Aunt Diane grabbed his arm and spun him. She was nursing a large black eye and a split lip. Abe took her into his arms and kissed her deeply, licking the blood off her lips. He pulled back and gazed into her eyes. "Fucking whore," he hissed with his mouth drawn back in disgust, and pushed her sprawling across the room then walked out, never looking back. A fond farewell.

Abe had laughed when he read about their murder-suicide. *Guess Uncle James had some balls after all*, he mused. His parents' home sat vacant, rightfully his, as was the world.

The water shut off. Abe waited patiently outside the bathroom door, but there was not a sound. Not a single bump, cough, or even scream. He knocked, the polite thing to do, then entered. The air hung heavy with hot steam. The floral-patterned curtain was still drawn across the shower. He looked down with disgust at her panties lying in the middle of the floor, then kicked them aside with his foot.

They began to dissolve into a muddy smear in the humid air. *What the hell?* he thought, stepping over the puddle of black from the slowly melting panties. It started to fill the cracks between the tiles. He drew back the curtain ... nothing. The shower stall was totally empty except for a strange odor. A smell that reminded Abe of the trash after it sat in the sun for a couple of days. He turned quickly, eyes darting to every corner of the small room. *Where is this bitch?* Then he saw the mirror. One word was written in the foggy mirror in a brown-edged smear.

MELT

Abe stared at the word, trying to comprehend. His mind was working scenarios out in his head, but they all were running short of an answer. He looked up at the ceiling, searching for a forgotten passage. He discounted this immediately, for there was no passage. Since her towel was still here, he couldn't imagine her being wet and nude in the two feet of blown fiberglass insulation above. She might be quiet but nobody could endure that in silence. He grabbed the towel and wiped the dripping letters on the mirror: they were more than written, the glass was etched deeply with grooves. Abe looked down at the basin edge and saw where the glass had dripped into small fragile buttons. A large bangle bracelet lay there encircling more of the brown stain dripping into the drain.

"What the hell did she slip me?" He spoke under his breath. "Yeah, that's it; fuckin' bitch musta given me something last night." He looked closely at the edge of the drain and touched the substance with the tip of his finger.

A slight sting quickly grew into an agonizing burning. Abe began to rub his finger on his shirttail and found it wasn't the best course of action. The skin from his fingertip flaked off. He yelled out. The pain was excruciating. *What is this shit?* he wondered, holding up his finger to examine. The movement dislodged his fingernail and it dropped to the tile floor. His eyes followed it, and then he noticed how the toe of his boot was slowly falling away exposing the steel toe where it had touched the long-gone panties. The nail melted away beside it. Abe quickly kicked the boot off. His finger was gone to the first joint, and showing no sign of slowing. Wide-eyed, holding his finger, he ran to the kitchen.

Abe had to push the cleaver the rest of the way through the bone of his finger. The cracking sound was louder than his cursing. The brownish liquid stopped as it reached the blade, before his finger slid away. A slight spray of blood stopped as Abe wrapped his hand tightly in a dish towel. He watched the stump of his missing finger as it spread out on the cutting board into a brownish goo. Amazed, he watched the small puddle begin to eat down into the wood cutting board. His lips moved as he tried to sort things out in his head. He looked at the towel in his hand blooming with blood and knew it needed attention first. Turning on the burner of the stove, he laid a knife in the flame. As the blade turned red, he unwrapped his hand, laying the heated blade against it. The pain and the stench made him vomit in the sink before he passed out.

He woke in ecstasy, lying on his back, loving when his aunt woke him this way. Abe stroked her head until his fingers entered the grey matter in the hole on the back of her skull. His eyes flew open as he pushed away ... nothing. A faint smell of her cheap perfume lingered in the air as his member, still wet with spit, became flaccid. Pushing himself up, he remembered the raw nerves on his hand and yelled out in pain as he fell back down. Cradling his hand to his chest, he used his free hand to pull himself up with a chair. A few strands of blonde hair were still in his grip, attached to a grey piece of scalp. Abe watched as they faded away. He laughed, calling out, "Okay, what did you give me?" No answer.

Oh, this bitch is gonna pay.

A low groan grew louder as Abe followed it back to the master bedroom. Entering, he stood slack-jawed at the figure sitting in the corner of the room. The groaning ceased as it noticed Abe. It was wearing red satin pajamas. With skin a sickening black, Uncle James lifted his gaze to Abe. His eyes, a milky grey color, seemed to be ready to escape their sockets and slide down his cheeks. A lone maggot crept out of his left eye and traveled down his face, looking like an obscene tear. Opening his mouth, the bottom lip drooped to the left and released a slow dark yellowish ooze that dropped noisily on his lap as he sat cross-legged.

"Bastard," he slurred, "I gave you everything." Then a loud belch escaped his mouth, making the yellow ooze drop off and filling the room with the stench of the grave.

"What the hell?" Abe's mind raced for sanity.

Uncle James chuckled, "You don't know what Hell is ... yet."

The maggot had found its way down and joined the flowing mucus, riding it to the growing puddle.

"You're dead!" Abe yelled as he reached for the bedside lamp to use as a club if necessary. Uncle James started to wheeze a laugh as he continued to spew foul fluids out onto his crossed legs.

"I always thought you were a smart one!" he groaned, trying to stand up. Uncle James was still cackling as his legs fell out from underneath him and his skin split and exploded into a soup of pus and maggots when he hit the floor.

Abe stepped back quickly as the wave of gore spread across the polished wood, filling the cracks and seeping down into the crawlspace.

The floor came alive as the boards were pounded from below. Sharp cracks and bumps vibrated on his bare feet. Abe retreated to the bed until the cord from the lamp in his hand pulled tight. The room went silent a second before the crawlspace door slammed open behind the closet door.

Abe stared as the ornate glass doorknob turned slowly and the door's hinges squealed lightly.

Her long beautiful red hair had not been marred by death. Though her head lay in an odd angle upon her shoulder, her green eyes were just as lovely as ever. Beneath the woman's nose, the skin hung loosely down around her exposed chin bone. The sight was almost comical with her lips lying in folds like a turtleneck sweater of skin. Abe could see where the plastic and duct tape she was so well encased in had been torn through, left dragging behind her as she stumbled out of the closet. Another cocoon of plastic was wiggling its way up from under the floor in the closet, behind the graying skin of her shoulder. He swung the lamp, only to be slowed mid-swing as the cord was unexpectedly pulled from the wall. It connected with her jaw, knocking her off balance.

Abe saw the progression of other plastic-sheeted phantoms working their way out of the closet. The sounds of the crackling plastic filled the room. Abe felt the bed sheet pull tight as her green eyes looked over the edge of the mattress, followed by her dislodged jaw hanging askew.

Abe screamed, closing his eyes, and waited. He opened them to an empty room with the closet door shut. No plastic. No red hair. No floor full of cocoons of death.

"No shit!" Abe laughed, slipping his foot to the floor and stopping abruptly as he felt plastic. He snatched his foot up and looked down until a hand stroked his back from the bed behind. He spun to see the girls, in different states of decomposition, leaning on their elbows. Those that had teeth and a face left smiled at him. The red-haired lady lay on the bed with her graying fingers and deep red nail polish pulling Abe down then straddling him. The others encircled the bed and held him as she leaned over his face, and from her broken mouth came a single drop of brown fluid.

He felt the sting immediately on his forehead. The tight skin melted off and exposed Abe's skull as the fluid burrowed deeper. Screaming when it melted away his eyelids, his last sight was her green eyes while his legs kicked out in spasms.

Abe opened his eyes. He could feel her breath on his back and he smiled in the comfort that she was still there. He woke several times in the night to reach back and feel her form, her heat, resting against his skin. He was sure madness would follow if she was gone ...

As it had happened before.

Patchouli

Patchouli. He breathed in again. Yes, definitely patchouli. Stu hadn't smelled that in a long time and it came back to him in a rush. The new tenant in the apartment next door brought the aroma to his senses. Stu admired her beauty when she was moving in, but as they first met her smell filled the air. Being proper, he introduced himself and shook her hand. Of course she smiled and offered her name, made some idle small talk. A few minutes passed, and she excused herself to tidy up her new place. As he shut the door to his apartment, he brought his hand to his face and closed his eyes then breathed deeply. Stu could see her green eyes and pink lips as he breathed. His other hand fumbled with his fly and soon he was masturbating furiously with his hand to his face, collapsing against the wall as he reached orgasm. He cried out her name while the waves of pleasure buckled his knees: Beth.

She didn't have visitors and she didn't go out at night. Stu felt a young lady of her age should be out partying, not cooped up in a small apartment, surrounded by the blue-hairs and their cats. The sound of Beth's soft music whispered through the air. He had moved a chair close to the wall that separated them. Often Stu would turn off the television and listen in the dark. He could imagine her body swaying to the beats of the music, her green eyes staring into his, and the patchouli.

He had heard it described as hippie perfume ... smelling like forest, pot, and snuggling. Stu found it mind-numbingly erotic. He had on several occasions waited for her to leave then followed behind her discreetly to enjoy the air, always ending up just inside his doorway pleasuring himself again. Her arrivals and departures were noted, so there was not an opportunity wasted — a chance to close his eyes and be with Beth again. He tried it at night in his bed, but the fresh scent of patchouli was the catalyst. It was strong.

Stu noticed a stain, coming through the wall. It enlarged as the days went by, and there was a definite smell. *Obviously, she had stacked some trash in the corner and forgot about it,* he reasoned. Stu needed to take care of this matter quickly, being the apartment handyman. He had spent many hours plunging toilets and painting empty apartments after tenants left. An organic stain like this would definitely be trouble trying to conceal. It would bleed through any paint he tried to conceal it with. He knocked on her door.

His heart raced thinking about entering her apartment, being alone with her. Stu's hands shook. He heard the music turn off. Stu knocked again.

"Beth?"

No answer. He knew she was home, heard her come in.

"Beth, are you okay?"

Again he was treated with silence. Perplexed, he went back to his apartment and wrote a note.

Hey Beth,
Noticed a stain coming through the wall. Perhaps you need help removing some trash? I'll come by later to get rid of it and fix the wall before it gets out of control.

Your handyman and neighbor,

Stu

He knocked once again and after a minute, slid

the note under the door. Pausing and listening with his ear cocked, he shook his head before walking back to his apartment. The phone rang as he entered. Mrs. Hammond on the second floor called to complain that the toilet was plugged up again. Her husband had died the year before. Since then, she always found things around her apartment to keep Stu busy at least once a week. Getting old was a lonely business. Stu grabbed the drain snake from a closet and stepped out his door. The hallway was silent except for the Johnson kids at the end of the corridor; they seemed to be in a bitter dispute about who had eaten the last doughnut. Unknown to them, their mother was enjoying the jelly-filled pastry at that very moment as she drove to work. Stu gave Beth's door another glance then bounded up the stairs to battle the fight of the porcelain.

Mrs. Hammond (call me Irene) didn't even attempt to be subtle in her quest to plug up the commode. Two washcloths and a quarter roll of toilet paper (still on the cardboard tube) were the offending objects. After placing the items in a plastic bag and rolling up the snake, he washed his hands. The older lady appeared at the door with a glass of lemonade.

"Now, Mrs. Hamm—," Stu began as the woman opened her mouth and raised a finger. "I mean, Irene." That seemed to appease her as she lowered her hand. "You can't be putting these things in the drain like that. They could plug up the pipes for the whole building."

"I have no idea what you're talking about, Stu. But while you are here, you might as well enjoy some lunch. It's the least I can do for a hard-working man." She gave a little wink and turned to the kitchen. He tried not to look but his eyes were drawn to her backside as she swayed in front of him. Stu smirked a bit at the sight of the deep panty lines prominently displayed in polyester. There was no use arguing about lunch; besides, he didn't have to pay for it or clean up afterwards.

She spoke intelligently and was quite a good conversationalist. Stu found himself engrossed in the subject until he spotted how the bread crumbs had collected in the corners of her mouth and it turned his stomach a little. He quickly excused himself, lying about another job he had to get to. Mrs. Hammond gave him a slightly dejected look and told him to come by anytime.

Stu,

I'm sorry about the trash! I've taken it to the dumpster. I have some errands to run, so just use your passkey and fix what is necessary in my place. Again I'm sorry and I will pay for the damage. I owe you a six-pack!

Beth

The note was taped to his door when he returned. She had just turned his note over and wrote on the backside. As he entered his apartment, Stu brought the note to his nose. The patchouli scent was strong and it stirred his loins. He went to the cabinet and grabbed a zip-lock bag to put the note into, then placed it on his nightstand for a later "use".

Stu dug out the passkey for her place from a hook board in the closet and went back to the hall. Turning the key in the lock, he nudged the door slightly with his shoulder. It swung open silently. The room was sparsely adorned with just the basics of furniture and drapery. He had needed to turn on the overhead light when he entered the gloomy room. Opening drapes, he found room-darkening shades on each window.

The smell in the room was an odd mixture of patchouli and something else. Stu couldn't place the stink, but he knew he didn't like it. He found the stain from the opposing wall to his room. It was triple the size on this side. He couldn't imagine she hadn't noticed it.

The light tan carpeting under the stain was immaculate, but Stu noticed it was recently laid back in place. The edges hadn't been pushed down correctly. He stomped the corners flat before painting the primer on the wall. He would have to come back later to paint again. The wallboard needed to be replaced when he had the materials, but this would do for now.

Standing, he noticed the large hook that was in the corner of the ceiling. It was the kind one would hang a bike from, certainly not a plant. She would leave a lot of work for Stu to do when moving out.

The scent of patchouli filled the room intensely. Stu closed his eyes and breathed in deeply; his head swam with pleasure. He went to the kitchen for a drink of water, amazed the fresh paint odor had already dispersed. Searching the cabinets for a glass, he found them completely empty. Stu opened the refrigerator and discovered that also was completely devoid of food. Only one item laid upon the wire shelf: a clear bag of burgundy fluid labeled with a red cross and a large O. He stared at it for a moment before closing the door. Gathering his tools, he let himself out.

A soft flow of jazz music floated in the air as Stu woke. Beth straddled his prone body with her hands beside his head, lips inches from touching, green eyes burning into his soul, her bare breasts gently brushing against his chest. *Yes,* he thought, *forever isn't long enough.* Treating him with a gift of a kiss, she forced something into his mouth with her tongue. Coughing and gagging, he tried to push her off. She held him down with the force of a vice. The leaves of a plant sprouted quickly from between his lips. Stu felt roots burrowing deep in his throat, little white flowers blooming under his nose; the smell of patchouli. He screamed himself awake, fingers clawing at his face, and threw up into his hands running to the bathroom.

As Stu's stomach settled, he pushed away from

the toilet seat. The memory of the dream ebbed like a tide, erasing the conscious footprints of fear. Angered, he opened his refrigerator and tossed the dinner leftovers of the night before. His first cup of coffee burned his throat as he swallowed. Vomiting was not a stranger to him. Bourbon and Stu had been quite good friends until the bottle was empty. He'd been dry, except for an occasional beer, for three months. Putting his head in the commode had been a real blast from the past; also a reminder that he needed to clean his toilet more often. The remnant of a six-pack stood upon the Formica counter with its plastic rings hanging limply from the one solitary can. Stu couldn't recall purchasing it. He stared into the floor, lost in thought, trying to piece the night before together.

Even if he had drunk five of them by himself, Stu didn't feel they would have left him unaware of his actions. He threw the last one in the garbage.

Beth knocked on his door in the late afternoon. She looked radiantly beautiful. Stu never realized her eyes were so green. She just amazed him. His knees grew weak when he saw the white flowers in her hair and smelled the patchouli.

"Stu, could you come finish that wall? I'm gonna be out of town for the weekend. I'd like to put this behind me before I leave." Beth flashed a blinding smile. Stu nodded; she could have asked for his kidney as far as he was concerned.

After collecting his tools, Stu rapped on her door. She had changed into a large terrycloth robe. Letting him in, Beth excused herself and went to the back room of the apartment. Stu soon heard the shower turn on. He listened intently as the sound changed when she entered, blocking the water from striking the backside of the tub. He could imagine it pelting her bosoms and running down her body. The handyman sighed deeply and turned to his work.

The drywall had slightly bubbled near the base, but he'd replace that in the future. Stu painted the wall with deliberate slowness, hoping to catch another glimpse of her. It was odd to him that he could see, in his mind, her naked body so clearly: down to the little freckle on her left breast. Putting the lid back on the paint can as the shower stopped its faint droning, Stu glanced down the hall. Feeling suddenly ashamed, he left her apartment.

While he was inserting the key in his door, Beth stuck her head out, hair still wet from washing.

"Stu?"

He looked over to meet her gaze. She was only wrapped in a towel. A stray drop of water ran down the bridge of her nose. "Yes, Beth?"

"All finished?" she asked as she wiped water from her face.

"Yeah, gonna have to replace part of that, but it's alright for now."

"Good. Can I get you to come back over in five minutes?"

Stu gave her adequate time to dress as he washed the paint out of the roller. Promptly in five minutes, he was tapping on her door. She opened it and held a fifty-dollar bill out to Stu.

The scent of the patchouli was strong.

"What's this for?" He stood with the crisp bill in his hand.

"For being such a great guy and taking care of my mistake." Beth flashed that smile that melted his heart again.

"Beth, I can't take money from ... "

And she closed the door.

Stu dreamed again that night. Beth laughed and teased him with the temptation of a kiss. But quickly pulled away when he drew her near; left him scratching his head.

Scratching ...

The scratching woke Stu from his torment. A definite scraping of something on the wall he had just fixed in Beth's apartment. There was a 'no pets' stipulation on the lease, and she had gone away for the weekend. Stu was sure she wouldn't leave an animal in the apartment alone. The sound stopped. He'd check out her place in the morning. Stu closed his eyes and hoped to dream of Beth again. He got his wish.

Daylight crept onto Stu's face; squinting from the intensity, he shielded his eyes. Every muscle in his body screamed out as he swung his legs to the floor. He hadn't been this sore since trying out a gym membership. Odd how being in her apartment the short periods of time, his skin smelled of patchouli also. Smiling, he reflected on the night. How she had given herself to him totally, and they had made love throughout the ... dream. Stu sighed deeply, and then limped to the shower.

Stu turned and pushed at Beth's door. It opened slightly then stopped abruptly, as the chain stretched its full length. Perplexed, he looked at his watch. She must have come home early in the middle of the night. Quietly he closed the door and locked it. Returning so late, she would be sleeping until the afternoon.

Mrs. Hammond called before lunch with her emergency of the week. One of the kitchen cabinet doors just fell off. She had all the screws in a dish on the counter when he arrived. Stu used his shoulder to hold weight while he twisted them back into the holes. With all his attention on the job, he felt a groping hand undoing his fly.

"Hey Ire ..." Looking down, it wasn't Mrs. Hammond's face staring up at him but Beth's. Stu watched as she fondled, then slowly fellated his growing member. He leaned back on the counter; as the smell of patchouli reached his nostrils, Stu reached climax. He almost fell from weak legs as the waves of pleasure pulsed through his body. Looking down to stare into the bright green eyes of Beth, he was instead treated to the satisfied smirk of Irene.

"You're always welcome to dessert after supper," she played with a wink. "And we're having spaghetti tonight."

Stu rushed back downstairs to his place. Feeling tired and a bit ill, he lay on his bed. The quietness was broken by scratching in the corner. Stu opened his eyes. The dim light of the room told him that it was evening. He looked at the clock and it was past nine. Feeling like he hadn't slept in days, the man stared into the dark corner concentrating on the scratching. Grabbing a bottle of water from the refrigerator, he emptied it in one tilt. Stu could feel cold spreading through his stomach. The corner grew quiet and soft Jazz filtered through the wall. He lay in bed listening to the familiar music; a soundtrack of a dream. The scent of patchouli filled his bed.

Sirens brayed outside his window. He threw on his robe and went into the hall. Pete Osten from an upstairs apartment walked over to Stu. Coming home from the bar, Pete had found Mrs. Hammond (call me Irene) crawling out her door. The neighbor called nine-one-one, but found her lying dead in a pool of her own vomit when he returned. He had heard the paramedics suspected poisoning.

"I think she did it to herself," Pete deduced. "Who would ever want to hurt a sweet old lady like that? Probably just missed her husband."

He watched as Irene was wheeled out with a sheet over her head. An orange stain spreading on the cloth. *Spaghetti,* Stu thought. Turning, he saw Beth standing at her door. She gave him a solemn look then stepped back. Stu could hear the chain sliding into place. He entered his apartment and took a long, hot shower. The water felt revitalizing; its thundering echo in the stall hid the scratching on the wall.

Stu woke with a maddening itch on his back. Sliding side to side on the sheets didn't help much, so he rubbed it on the corner of the door. It subsided after ten minutes. His thirst was monumental. He drained two water bottles as he stood at the refrigerator door.

A police detective knocked as he was cooking breakfast. Just formalities, asking questions about Mrs. Hammond and her guests. Stu told him about fixing her cabinet the day before, but left out the other occurrence. *The cop didn't need to know everything. Besides, how could that have anything to do with poisoning?* Stu reasoned. The officer wrote notations in a little book before replacing it inside his breast pocket. Smelling the air, he took out the pad again and made some more marks. The detective thanked Stu and left a card in case "anything else came to mind".

The Hammonds' son drove down from his home upstate; Stu let him into her apartment. The police had removed all the houseplants from the place. They said the poison had been botanical in nature. The son assured Stu that his parents' belongings would be out within a week. After giving condolences he left, not wanting to remember the last time in the kitchen. Or how he had wanted to return for spaghetti, feeling guilty about the enjoyment she had given him as she swallowed his orgasm. Stu rushed home and drank another bottle of water. His thirst seemed endless.

Beth's eyes didn't look as green and her skin lacked any luster. Stu passed her in the hall. She hadn't said a word.

"Um, Beth?" he stammered. "You okay?"

She flashed a slight smile; it wasn't as enchanting. "Yeah, fine." She slid her key in the lock. "Stu, could you come by later? I need some help moving something."

"I have time now."

"No, give me a couple of hours first. My apartment's a mess and I'd rather you not see it that way." She opened the door and locked it behind her.

Stu sat in the tub with the water up to his neck. He had to turn the tap on a few times, as he gulped his bathwater.

Beth answered the door before his knuckles rapped a second time. Her eyes gleamed bright green again. Stu was amazed every time he saw her, how much she affected him. The overhead light was off and candles were strewn about the room. He looked over to the corner. The carpet was pulled back again; the floor beneath it was covered with plastic as was the wall. A decaying, swampy odor hung in the air, with the strong scent of patchouli. A green, gelatinous pod hung from the hook, pulsating and swaying as if it was alive. The bottom stalk curved up and scraped the wall with each swing. It was long and narrow, expelling a line of ooze that glistened yellow in the dim candlelight.

"What the hell is ... ?" Stu's question was cut short as Beth locked the door. He turned to push his way past her. She had disrobed and was standing naked behind him. Her hands lifted the bottom of his shirt over Stu's head. He breathed shallowly as she pulled down his pants leaving him bare. Beth grabbed his erection and led him down the trail of candles to the bathroom. The tub was full and he did not need to be told to get in. The water felt incredible. Beth left the doorway for a moment, then returned. She was carrying the pod.

He was drinking the water when he realized what she had. It smelled awful. But the smell of the patchouli in the water masked the odor well. The pod twisted in her hands, leaving a gelatin film. She brought her fingers to her lips and sucked them clean. Her eyes glowed a deeper green in the candlelight.

"Sorry, Stu," Beth began. "I need this to live, and it needs you. The only thing it eats is the patchouli oil, but the plant must be grown in a human body."

She slid the pod into the tub with him. Stu could feel it probing his body until it found his penis, and a jolt of pain ran through him as it latched on.

"I had cultivated your body and seeded the harvest. I want to thank you for keeping it so well irrigated, but I see poor Mrs. Hammond didn't care for the taste. Now it must feed on you to make my food."

Waves of pleasure paralyzed Stu in the tub. The ecstasy he felt outweighed the horror. Sprigs of white flowers broke the surface of the water, as the pod twisted and fed.

Beth smiled, rubbing the ooze on her hands all over her breasts. She reached in as the pod floated to the top of the water and carried it to the hook in the living room. It was swollen after feeding. Lucky it only needed to eat every seven years. Beth reached in the bathtub and let the water swirl down the drain. A layer of white flowers covered the bottom. She lay down on the living-room floor below the pod as it twisted and purged a layer of vomit on Beth. She massaged it in with glee.

God, she was beautiful.

Takers

My mind screams to stop as my boy, my son cries out "Daddy!" Soon his blood floods my throat, quenching the thirst and needs of these parasites that have taken me. His dead body held in the arms that used to be mine. Though my pain and anguish are still my own. These accursed things haven't stopped me from thinking. My mind burns in hatred of myself, of these creatures. I'd hoped I could have been stronger, could have pushed away and fought the paralysis of free will. Yet the agonizing moments of taking my son's life cannot stay my hand or my teeth. My stomach churns as they feed, releasing their hold on me. My stomach warm with blood, my movements become my own again. They are still in there waiting. I can feel them moving.

I had taken my family to the beach to enjoy a day in the sun. The kids' last hurrah before school would return them to the drudgery of reading, 'riting, and 'rithmetic. They both were decent students with different strengths and weaknesses in subjects. After months of summer vacation, the mood around the house had been low. I understood, remembered being a kid too.

Ann, my wife, had purchased a cute little bikini for this outing. As with many couples, our love life had suffered through the years. Being Mom and Dad always came first. Most times we found for each other seemed hurried and sometimes without passion, just going through the motions. But today, I found myself ogling her quite often. The strings on the sides of the panties tied in perfect bows that could come undone with a simple tug. I fought the urge to do so, for now. Childbirth had been kind to her body.

It was a piece of private beach on the Gulf owned by my company. We had used it a few times over the years. A small stretch of sand separated from the access road by a rusty fence, and dunes that swayed with life as the grasses blew in the breeze. Even though it was a fifty-mile drive, the seclusion was worth it. One could look across the water until it disappeared on the horizon, a line only blemished by the small cresting waves. Funny how the curve of the Earth makes things seem to disappear and show us how small we really are. Closing my eyes, I could feel the problems of life slipping away. Yeah, it was a good day.

Eric splashed his sister at the water's edge. Julie, being four years his senior at the ripe-old-age of twelve, yelled at him and then glared in our direction with an irritated look in her eyes. I smirked and peered back over my shoulder to Ann. She was bent into the trunk of the car digging the towels and sunscreen out from beneath the coolers. Her bikini bottoms, decorated with an orange and red sunburst pattern, bounced beautifully filled with her tight derriere. Damn, she looked great. I glanced down and slid my hand over my expanding gut and made a mental note to start a regime of sit-ups.

"Hey, it's my vacation too," Ann pointed out. "Can you give me a hand here?"

I gazed at her and grinned. "With pleasure, Milady, with pleasure."

We laid out a blanket on the white sands. Judy lay on a beach towel in her dark sunglasses, covered with coconut suntan lotion, the smell broadcasting on the breeze. A small radio positioned near her belted out Top Forty music from the local station. The tide, which on our arrival was fifty feet away, crept ever closer as the day passed. Eric had built a sandcastle when we first arrived that was now being swallowed up and restructured by nature. A multitude of ham-and-cheese sandwiches were consumed and most of the soda. One can sprayed Julie in a small geyser. Total shock played across her face as it dripped off her chin. Eric began to laugh. What can I say? It was contagious. I laughed heartily also. Julie, finally comprehending the moment, giggled herself after a few glimpses of our smiles.

"Dad, can I go back in the water?" Eric pleaded, his eyes looking like one of the stupid starving animal paintings that had hung on my wall as a child.

I reached down and ruffled his hair. "Go ahead. I think Julie needs to rinse off anyways. But those are some bad storm clouds on the horizon. So it won't be long." The last part of this statement was said loudly across the beach to his backside. I looked up at the clouds again. I didn't care for them one bit. Dark black thunderheads followed by a sky of grey. Damn, they were moving fast too. I was thinking about the drive home in the oncoming weather. Hopefully it would pass quickly.

"Hey, Slugger." Ann had come up behind and wrapped her arms around me. I could feel her skin against my back. She looked across the water at the children and slid her hand down. "I noticed you looking, and I want you to help me take off this thing when we get home." I turned and kissed her deeply. *My pleasure, Milady, my pleasure.*

A loud thud on the beach mere yards from where we were standing. The object looked like a huge flesh-colored coconut lying next to the small pit created as it fell from the sky. Hissing, it vented steam from an enlarging crack on the side of the projectile.

"What is it?' Ann questioned, just as several more thumps and splashes brought my attention to the children in the water. Eric stood knee-deep as the tempo of the falling objects increased. Julie was already running up the beach screaming, holding her hands above her head. One of those things fell in front of her, diverting her course. One had fallen atop the radio and silenced it forever.

"Get her in the car!" I yelled back at Ann, but she had already grabbed Julie by the hand and headed that way. I scanned the waves until my eyes rested on Eric. He was paralyzed in fear as the pods plummeted in the surf all around him. I ran straight to him, feeling one of those things slide down my back as it fell. It burned like hell. As I reached the water, I noticed the ones in the water were split open. The tide squirmed with black worms.

"Eric, come straight to me!" My son's eyes met mine and it broke him out of his stupor. I could see those damned worms sliding up his legs, and I dashed for him. Lifting him into my arms as eyeless obscenities bumped my legs, I twisted and ran towards the car. The water held my feet in a slow-motion effect as we made our way out of the ocean. I hadn't seen the split-open pod float in front of me, and it sent me sprawling. The momentum of the fall propelled Eric onto the beach, whereas I fell face-first into the water. It was thick with black worms. I could feel them bouncing off my face as I tried to stand. One had attempted to burrow its way into my left nostril, wiggling and squirming. I reached up and grasped it and snatched the thing out. Then I felt it. They had swam into my shorts, found *another* access point. I stood up quickly and reached into my trunks just a moment too late. I'm sure it was just the one, but I can feel it moving.

Eric stood on the beach looking back at me. "Run!" I screamed as we both began to dodge the craters in the white sands.

My wife held the door open as we slid into the backseat. The rain of pods increased again, and the roof of the car bent down lower upon our heads while the glass cracked in a spider-web fashion. Ann held Julie's head to her bosom as the girl cried out in fear. Eric held my hand tightly. And, dammit ... I could feel it moving inside me.

"Get us out of here!" I yelled.

"I can't, the keys are out there." My eyes followed the direction of her finger. The keyring with WHO'S YOUR DADDY? painted on a four-inch plate lay next to the blanket half covered with sand, the word DADDY face up to the sky. Ten feet away; might as well have been a mile.

"I'll get them!" Ann yelled, opening the door.

"No!" I bellowed. But she was already out the door and grabbing the keys. She tossed the keyring into the car as she slid back inside. Then her body lurched. I could see one of those pods falling away amid a spray of blood and brains. Julie screamed as Ann's body rolled off the seat half out the door with her legs still in the car. Her bright red toenails, fresh from a pedicure, were now hanging over the top of the seat.

"Julie, you gotta get us out of here! I can't get to the front!"

"But ... Mom!"

I grasped Ann's foot and shoved it out the door. "Now slide over and put the key in the ignition or we are all gonna die!" She trembled violently, attempting to maneuver the keys, but she did really well — even when I felt the car run over Ann's body. As we passed the dunes, it was evident that this wasn't a localized thing. The landscape was covered with pods.

"Where now?" Julie turned back to look at me. I wasn't ready to answer, because I didn't know. A pod crashed into the windshield, caving it in slightly. Julie screamed and sobbed loudly.

"Wait, I see something!" She stomped the gas. I could only guess that it wasn't the road she had taken, a straight course to wherever she was driving. I was thrown toward the roof on several occasions as Julie tested the suspension on the car. A loud crack. The rear of the car dropped and dragged on the ground behind. She pushed the gas harder; the engine roared. I could see a building ahead and thought we might make it, until the wheels dug into the sand then began to spin. She didn't stop pushing the gas.

"Julie! Julie! Stop!" I yelled over the screaming engine. I put my hand on her shoulder. I could see so much fear in her eyes.

"NO! We can't stop, we're almost there!" The pods still rained slowly around us. I looked at the building. Maybe 200 yards away, across the road. The projectiles that fell to the lane had all split open. The space between the structures was alive with movement. I could see a large dog in front of the building eating something on the ground. Then it noticed us. As it slowly approached, I could see it was a black lab with its bloated belly writhing. The dog walked to my window with tail wagging, then threw itself at the glass. It bounced off and fought to stand back up. The window was almost laying into the car now covered with black hair and blood. One more of those attacks and he would be in the backseat.

"Eric, climb over into the front seat. When I say go, I want both of you to get out the passenger door and run as fast as you can to the building. I'll be right there, I promise. Don't look back." He did as I asked, then they both stared at me as I reached for the door handle. "Now!" I yelled and pushed open the rear door. The dog climbed right in. I could hear the kids running; I brought the seatbelt up. Worms flopping out of its mouth, I wrapped the belt around its neck and pulled it as tight as I could. A collar identifying the dog as SK dug into my wrist while I squeezed. I heard its neck snap, and it went limp in the seat. Before I slid out, I could tell something was different. There were more of them. I could feel them moving.

Julie screamed. I ran on those worms barefoot. The ground was slick and I almost lost my footing. Both children had made it to the building. An old sign hung above a dented door: *AL'S GARAGE.* A large man lay in the street where the dog had been eating. His coveralls, stained with oil, identified him as Al by a name-patch. His face was gone. I hit the door running; it slammed hard and the knob embedded itself into an interior wall. My eyes tried to scan the room but hadn't yet adjusted to the dimness. I heard scuffling in front of me and was hampered from doing anything by the lack of sight. I grabbed a passing figure and pulled it into the light. It was a large middle-aged woman. She spun around and treated me to the business end of a shotgun.

"Hold on!" I shouted.

"Mister, I don't know what's going on here, but my husband is dead and I've got something running around the inside of my garage!"

The barrel of the gun shook feverishly as she tried to keep her composure. Then she looked beyond me, and raise the weapon, and fired. The blast was so close to my ear, I fell in pain against the door. Al tumbled down across me. The shot had blown out half his chest away, and black worms squirmed from the wound. His grease-stained overalls stank of oil and perspiration. What was left of his face rolled down my shirt, his teeth catching on the fabric. With great effort, I crawled away as the black slimy bastards fell out of the gory mess that once was Al, onto my bare legs. My head ringing with pounding pain, I found my way back to an upright position. Reaching up, I felt the warmth of blood dripping slowly out of my left ear. Other than a constant high-pitched squeal, it was totally useless.

The woman wore a mask of grief, staring down at the faceless corpse by my feet. She didn't offer any resistance when I took the shotgun from her. I turned and pushed the re-deceased man out of the entryway with my feet as I held the frame for balance. The slime the worms left everywhere made this task a bit easier. He simply slid on a layer of mucus until I was able to shut the door. Light from outside illuminated the threshold, with shadows of the worms creeping underneath. From my good ear, I could hear the lady blubbering behind me. The tin roof was still playing a thunderous melody that seemed to shake even the air of the building as an unknown amount of pods fell from the heavens. I felt a hand clasp mine and looked down to see Eric's face, eyes wide with fear.

"Where's your sister?" My eyes were acclimating to the gloom slowly. He pointed to a far corner. I squinted in the dark until I could see her outline coming toward me. Julie fell into my arms sobbing, her breathing in hitches. I felt so helpless. Holding tight as her body shook in fear, twitching every time the roof deflected another projectile. Eric stomped on the worms that were writhing on the cement floor. Tears flowed from his eyes but he was silent. I found the light switch and flicked it on. The room filled with the harsh glow of the fluorescent tubes. Walls lined with tool boxes and various pieces of equipment flanked two bays, the closest empty. The other contained a late model truck in obvious disrepair. The pounding on the roof stopped altogether.

Behind us the woman began to giggle. I turned to see her sitting on the floor. Several worms had climbed up her body and were at the edge of her lips. "They kinda tickle." Her eyes were locked onto mine, the worms filling her mouth. I could see the poor lady's throat swell as they fought to delve deeper. Hands clawed at her neck in an attempt to breathe. Face deepening in color, she fell prone on the floor. The things swarmed — finding any place to climb up on her or, even worse, in her. She groaned and twitched just as the door opened. A shadow passed over the threshold, too small to be Al. A form familiar, yet different.

"Mom?" Julie yelled and ran to her. I couldn't stop her in time. The car had driven over Ann's midsection and forced the internal organs lower into her abdomen, giving her a horrific silhouette. She fell upon Julie as the girl reached her. The side of her head was misshapen and adorned with dried blood and brains. But her teeth worked all too well. Eric cried out. I brought the shotgun up and froze. I died a thousand times in that moment. And I squeezed ... nothing happened but an audible click. Cursing myself, I jacked the spent shell out and pumped a fresh round into the chamber. I fired. It impacted Ann between her shoulder blades, throwing the body three feet away.

Her legs kicked in death throes, knocking over several pipes leaning against the wall, until she seemed to regain something within and stood back up.

I looked down at Julie. Her throat was ripped out, and the worms were having no problem making themselves a new home. Eric was wailing uncontrollably. Ann turned and stumbled back towards me. Her once-beautiful skin was now marred by the cursed day's events. The side of her head had become concave. And her left eye bulged amid a bed of gray matter, forced out of its socket. I pumped the gun then fired again. It played out in front of me like slow-motion when her body flew back. Her wounds made a wide crimson trail of gore sliding down the wall as she fell in a heap with the damned black things coursing through the new holes. Eric screamed.

My paralysis was broken by the large lady behind me, just as her teeth sank into my shoulder. Pain telegraphed through my arm, causing me to drop the gun. Her face, so close to my ear, grunted and chortled while her teeth came together removing a bite of flesh. I fell to my knees as she chewed, my blood lining the edges of her mouth. Her hunger obviously not sated, she bore down upon me teeth first. The shotgun barrel caught her in the neck, breaking through her trachea. I squeezed the trigger and again was treated with the firing pin striking an empty chamber. Her weight pressed down. Uncaring that the firearm was embedded deep into her neck, she gnashed her teeth mere inches from my face. Her breath reeked of some ungodly stench. My body slipped on the amassing slime and goo on the floor, trying to push her away. Coffee-stained incisors scraped the skin of my cheek, just as Eric buried a tire iron into the bitch's back.

She screeched an inhuman sound before rolling off, attempting to reach the tool protruding from between her shoulder blades. I snatched the shotgun free of the gaping hole in her neck, pumped a load into the chamber and fired. The head stayed attached to her body by strings of sinew. All other movement ceased except for the parasites fleeing their host. They poured out of the wounds in an almost fluid motion.

My gut knotted in pain, the invaders of my body let me know they were there. I fell against a rack of mufflers until the intensity diminished. Eric stood over the lady's remains and retrieved his weapon. The black tool slid out effortlessly. The face I looked into had changed so much from the child who ran into the surf just a short time earlier. His eyes no longer held the twinkle of youth. I watched in awe and horror as he marched to his sister's now-rising body and cleaved her skull with the tire iron. He swung the steel repeatedly and her head turned to pulp. I grabbed his swinging arm and he growled, actually bared his teeth at me, then surrendered to the terror as tears flowed from his eyes. The weapon clanged to the cement floor as Eric clutched onto my mid-section. I felt such despair over losing my family. The floor still ran thick with the black bastards, which no longer aimed to climb onto us but wiggled into the darkness of the garage.

Eric lifted his head, and in the meager fluorescent lighting we exchanged a last glance of love. My son; he will never know the joy of fatherhood. Never know the touch of a woman or the heartbreak of love. I had failed him. My arms cradled his head tightly. My mind screamed out to stop. Eric cried, "Daddy!" And with a quick twist the deed was done. The sound echoed in the garage as his neck broke.

The floor is bare except for the bodies. My movements have stayed my own since feeding on my son. Such a cruel fate to not be able to control your actions yet be conscious of them all. The worms must be multiplying in my gut; it grows distended. They twist and turn and grow hungry. The last shell of the shotgun is firmly seated in the chamber. The barrel under my chin, I stop and weep until there is a surge of movement deep inside, like they know what is going to happen. A final tear doesn't have time to fall before my face evaporates.

Funny ... I can still feel them moving.

Tears of Love

"Shhh! Dammit, be quiet!" Charles looked back at me with a scowl on his face. "Dad will be plenty pissed if he catches us."

Now I wish our father had caught us.

My parents became really watchful since my sister Amy disappeared last year. Mom had said Amy was hanging out with the wrong people. Dad doesn't discuss her at all; Amy was his princess, his little girl. Once, I walked in on him watching old videos of Amy sitting on his shoulders when she was really young. The father on the video smiled and laughed; the father I was left with got drunk and yelled at me with red eyes and stinky breath. I felt cheated.

Charles was always so adventurous and I, his younger brother by two years, just wanted his attention. I would have followed him to Hell. Last night I did. God, I loved him.

We escaped from the house without incident. As usual, I was following three steps behind Charles. I found trying to keep up with him harder than ever before since his legs had gotten longer this summer. He may have been only twelve, but in my eyes he was so cool.

When Charles slowed up to let me walk by his side, he glanced over at me and smiled.

"Picks said it was over in the drainage culvert near the old Theine house. He said he heard his brother talking about it." I rolled my eyes thinking it had to be Picks.

Joey Picks is a complete idiot. His actual name is Pikes, but after a booger-picking incident in the school locker room, he would always be known as Picks. Yep, he was knuckle-deep. He became the school joke in the lunchroom. "Hey Picks, that s'not dinner!" I laughed real hard when I heard this one the first time. Dang, it was so funny.

Some say Joey's brother Tim is into devil worship. He walks around town wearing weird makeup and black clothes. I think Amy had a crush on him. Charles teased her about a necklace Tim Pikes had given her, it was some kind of star dangling from a leather string, and she turned red and slammed her bedroom door. A week later she disappeared.

Last week I was walking in town and saw Tim sitting in his black van staring at me. I could see a hint of red underneath the bad paint job, and he had covered the back windows with cardboard and duct tape. Charles said he'd caught Tim watching him too. Mom had said he just got out of jail for vandalizing the cemetery; really gave me the willies! Knowing Tim, if he said there was a girl's body in the ditch, well, maybe it was true.

The Theine house was just creepy. It didn't appear that much different from the other houses in the area. But no kids ever dared to walk up the crumbling sidewalk to the front door. There were rumors of sounds inside the house, rumors of kids disappearing, and after the Johnston's dog was found dead next to the back door, there were rumors of vampires. The Golden Retriever didn't have any blood left in its body. The vet burned the dog quickly in fear of it spreading a disease. It had howled in the flames ... how does anything dead howl? Well, that's what I'd heard.

Our neighbor Tommy Soames said he once went to the door of the Theine house on a bet. He said there was scratching on the other side of the door. I told him it was probably just a dog that was trying to get out. He glared at me. "I heard laughing. Dogs don't laugh."

Tommy would always take a dare. Heck, once he had even slapped Old Lady Jimes on the butt as she bent over in the library. This was different, it really scared him. He was so serious. I just punched him in the arm and smiled. He didn't smile back. It wasn't like Tommy to be spooked, but that house creeped him out in a way I never thought possible.

"C'mon Spud, keep up."

I remember the day Charles began calling me that. Mom had been trimming a piece of bubble gum that had tangled into my hair in my sleep, and then she'd spotted my ears.

"Could grow potatoes in those ears," she scolded. Charles laughed and Mom gave him a stern look. He gave me a little punch in the arm and snickered, "Let's go shoot some hoops, Spud."

After that I kept my ears really clean in hopes that he'd stop calling me such a stupid name. Now I wish he was around so I could hear him say it again; especially as I remembered last weekend.

Charles and I spent the whole day fishing for brim at the old quarry. We tried to do that trip once a month. I think we enjoyed the time alone, just being ourselves with each other. Heck, I'd even gotten used to cussing a little around him on these trips. He'd scold me a bit and tell me to watch my mouth, and then we'd both laugh at how stupid some of it really sounded. The fish were biting pretty well that day and soon we had quite a few in our bucket.

"Spud, why don't ya get some sticks so we can cook these things up," Charles suggested, so I began searching the area for loose wood. After a few minutes I had enough to start a fine fire. I ran to his side to watch as he began gutting our catch, their severed heads in a small pile at his feet. I pushed on the fish eyes with my finger and marveled at how cool they felt.

"Hold this." He held out the knife to me; handle first, just like Daddy had taught him. It felt heavy in my hands, at least six inches unfolded and sharp. I wiped the small line of fish blood from the blade on my tee-shirt. Charles rolled his eyes and continued his work pulling the guts out of our lunch with his fingers. I folded up the blade and handed it back to him before we cooked our catch on sticks over the fire. They were always burnt on the outside and raw on the inside, but it was always the best lunch brothers ever shared.

"The Theine house is clean across town," I stated. "Why didn't we ride our bikes?" Actually I was glad we weren't riding, but heck I was ten. I had to do some whining.

"Dad woulda heard us for sure if we opened the garage." Charles looked over at me and patted my belly. "Looks like you could walk off some of that jelly roll, anyway." I swatted his hand away and we both laughed.

There was a perfect crescent moon in the night sky and the road was dimly lit. There were a lot of shadows. In the daytime I had walked these roads for hours on end. If I hadn't been with Charles, I would've been rapidly running back home.

I reached up and touched the tail of his shirt, a dark red flannel he had worn so often. He looked at me and I snatched my hand back in embarrassment. Charles smirked at me as I stared at him.

He knew I was scared. Hiking across town to see a dead girl sounded like an awesome road trip in Charles's room earlier. Now as we walked, I thought to myself … *Well, I'm sure Picks was lying.* I kinda hoped he was. Goosebumps covered my arms, and I could feel them make their way down my legs.

We traveled along a row of houses, each with their manicured lawns and chain-link fences. The links chimed, "Ting, ting!" as I ran my fingers over them. Suddenly a big Rottweiler bounded at one of the fences, snapping and growling. The whole fence rang as the dog hit it. I let out a slight yelp.

"Cripes, Spud," Charles commented, "think ya dropped a dauber in your shorts!"

"Aww, shut up!" I shot back, fully realizing he was almost right. *A brave adventurer cuts his journey short by crapping his pants.* I hurried up and positioned myself so Charles was between me and the fence line.

We walked that way without conversation for at least two miles. I could see the Theine house in the distance, beckoning us forward. The promise of a dead girl held out like bait.

"What do ya think she looks like?" I asked, trying to act tough.

"Probably all bloated and black," Charles said. "Might stink to high heaven, too!" I hadn't thought of the smell; I could feel my stomach knotting up.

"Why would her body still be there?"

Charles stopped and turned to me. "I don't know, it just is."

Who could argue with that? I shrugged my shoulders at my own thought. It was a logic I couldn't dispute.

As I looked ahead I could see the shirttail of Charles's red flannel waving in the light breeze, the moonlight making it greyer then red. He was on a mission, heading to the house with all the stealth a twelve-year-old could muster. I was following behind, jealous of his courage.

We reached the culvert with wide eyes and hope. It was a deep ditch, probably ten feet down with a concrete pipe running under the road. Standing water in the swell covered the bottom of the pipe. It smelled like the bathroom after Dad left it with his newspaper tucked under his arm.

"Awww man," I griped, "there's nothing here." My shoulders slumped with the realization that just an hour before I had thought Picks was an idiot, and now it looked like I was right.

"Wait, I see something," Charles whispered. And edged his way closer.

Then I saw it too: a white hand, just under the surface of the water at the rim of the culvert. I looked over at Charles, no more than five feet away, as he headed down the steep embankment.

"Charles, c'mon, we've seen it," I begged -- feeling the sudden need for home; for Mom, for Dad, for the safety of my own bed.

"We didn't come all the way here to chicken out," Charles said. "I just want to see her face."

As he turned around, the hand slipped back into the darkness of the concrete pipe.

"Crap!" Charles exclaimed. "What happened?"

He looked up at me, but my eyes looked past him at the two hands that gripped both sides of the pipe behind him. She was pulling herself out. Her long stringy hair hung down in her face as her eyes met mine. Charles turned and saw her as his feet gave way under the gravel of the steep side.

She was out of the pipe to her hips now, and she was nude. Even in the moonlight I sensed a strong familiarity to her shape. I stared until my eyes widened in total recognition.

I couldn't believe it!

"Run, Spud!" Charles shouted as he scrambled up the embankment. He was at the top when she leapt next to me. I looked up into her eyes and she touched my chin with those cold fingers. I raised my gaze to hers. I was lost in those eyes, and I wanted to stay there. I could only stare as her mouth opened to reveal her white perfect fangs. A wonderful cinnamon smell filled the air.

Charles hit her in a run. I stood stunned as I watched him get up from the naked form on the wet grass. He grabbed my hand and we ran toward the only structure around, our only haven, the Theines house.

The front porch light was on; the house had been totally dark when we first arrived at the ditch. I don't believe either one of us cared where we were when we mounted the porch, we were that scared. I stared as she seemed to glide toward us then hid my eyes in Charles's flannel shirt while he tried the door and pushed, giving us access to the dim entryway.

I looked up at Charles, who slammed the door and threw the thumb lock. He was crying. I hugged him tightly, breathing hard, as the pounding on the door began only a foot from where we huddled. He reached over and slapped at the wall a few times until he found a light switch that was next to the door.

A hanging lamp above flooded the room to the left. Through the dust that danced around the bulb, I could make out several moving figures before the light fizzled and the laughter began. The sound became a sweet song playing in my ears. I knew Charles heard it too, because he loosened his grip on me.

"Please don't let go, Charles, please," I begged.

In the dim light from between the door frame, I could see his hand reaching for the thumb lock again. The door burst in as the old door jamb splintered, almost stabbing me in the gut with a sharp board. The entryway was lit up from the porch light until a silhouette filled the frame.

Charles pushed me behind himself as he glared at the ghoul, his fists balled tightly. Then his eyes widened and he smiled at her in recognition. She touched his face with her hand. Laying his head on her chest, my brother looked completely at peace.

She was beautiful once, my sister Amy. I remember that sophomore picture my parents used on her missing posters. Amy had come home from a date one night shivering with the cold. The next morning she had a bad fever. She never told us who she was with that night or where she'd been.

I had gone in to see her; she'd trembled so hard it shook her bed. Amy's dark hair spilled across the pillow, a true contrast to her pale face. As I watched, not knowing what to do, her bed stopped shaking. I ran to get Mom, but when I got back Amy's bed was empty. No one knew where she had gone.

Now Amy glared at me, snarling as she sank her teeth into the nape of Charles's neck.

"No!" I cried, reaching for him as he drooped in her arms. I could hear her sucking and some blood escaped her lips, trickling down his neck.

Out of the darkness, nightmarish creatures escaped the gloom and began to crawl to my feet. If those things had ever been human, they no longer showed any signs of it; they slid on stumps, their entrails dragging behind them. Misshapen skulls with bulging eye sockets, their teeth sharpened to points, gnashed at the air. Skinless muscles stretched over their bodies, mostly covering the bones, but not totally. I screamed and they began a chorus of laughter, an obscene noise that still haunts my mind.

As they advanced, they left a trail of gore. The closest extended its black, bloated tongue as if to taste the floor below. I kicked out my foot to stop its approach. The blow caught the beast under its jaw, severing the tongue and spraying blood across the bottom of my jeans. This brought a renewed round of laughter as the tongue inched its way into the darkness.

I fixed my eyes on Amy, still holding my brother in one arm. She joined in with the laughter. I saw right then how truly ugly she had become. Her soul, if she could even have one, was black.

Charles, still with a smile of contentment on his face, opened his eyes. His blood was making a large half-moon stain on the collar of his shirt. He looked directly into my tear-filled eyes and his smile vanished. His eyes studied mine, then widened; his hand slipped into his pocket. I knew instantly what he was reaching for.

"Run, Mike!" Charles yelled, as his hand came from his pocket with the knife. Flicking it open, he arched for Amy's neck. I saw the blade flash in the porch light before he thrust it in her throat.

Amy dropped Charles to clasp the knife. I heard him cry out in pain when one of the creatures gleefully bit down on the hand he used to break his fall. Amy screeched, pulling the knife out of her throat. A black, empty hole remained in her neck with a flap of skin loosely covering the space.

The stainless steel blade hummed past my ears as I turned. When I reached the top step of the front porch, I could feel her cold fingers touching the back of my neck. I pushed off with a leap. Falling down hard on that broken sidewalk with tears streaming from my eyes, I heard Charles grunt.

Two bodies fell beside me where I lay. Amy opened her mouth in a soundless scream as Charles pushed a piece of the door frame he'd hung on to deep into her back. Her lips receded from crumbling teeth, until her skin dried and blackened. Her body collapsed in upon itself. The hellish laughter became screams as the other creatures pulled away from the doorway, retreating into the shadows.

Charles stood and reached his hand to mine. Painfully realizing he was missing most of his fingers, he held out the other hand to help me up.

I stood crying as he stared back into the gloom of the house. "Go home, Spud, I've gotta finish here." Then he walked into the doorway with his makeshift stake in his hand. I started after him to stop him, but he yelled at me to go home and pushed the door closed on its broken frame. I climbed the first step and heard Charles scream out in agony. I fell to my knees and landed on the knife. I grabbed it and shoved it into my pocket, then got up just as the hideous laughter started over, and Charles's screaming became louder. Sobbing, I turned and ran, never looking back, until I was surrounded by silence, except for the sound of my feet slapping the roadway and my sobs into the night. I cried at the horrors I'd seen, and the loss of Amy, again, and mostly Charles, my brother ... my friend.

The van was parked a short distance from the house. I could see the red tip of a cigarette in the darkness of the driver's side window as I passed; I heard the door open with a creak. My heart pounding, I ran into the thick brush off the side of the road. Dropping down onto my belly, I hid under a bush, its pointy branches stabbing me in the side. Hitching in fear, I held my breath. Coughing, Tim tromped by me and hocked a loogie. It had landed on my left hand.

I waited there; I could hear him wading back to the road through the thick weeds. I nearly jumped as a rabbit came out of the brush three feet from my face. It looked at me and without fear hopped away. I stayed still until only the sounds of the crickets were all around me. I was alone now.

The moon hid lazily, half obscured by the low clouds, but still bright enough for me to see as I walked quickly the rest of the way home. It was clear what I needed to do.

I slipped into the garage and found Charles's tackle box. I stuffed the matches in my pocket then waited until dawn and began my trip back to that hell-spawned house. As I got close, I could see Tim's black van parked in front of the Theine place. I could see him closing the rear door of the vehicle. I stayed out of sight until he drove away.

The old wood burned like tinder. I watched for an hour as the structure collapsed in upon itself, leaving a fiery pit in its forgotten basement ... burning everything ... hopefully everything. There were no sirens; no firemen came to the rescue. It just burned, unnoticed and without a moan or scream. The house just died. My childhood died with it.

Oddly, there was a little smoke coming out of the culvert. My mind raced; there had to be a passage here from the house. I sat on the edge of the ditch as I watched a bloodied red flannel shirt floating at the edge of the concrete pipe. I stared at it and my heart hurt.

I knew.

That's where they found me, watching a cloud of smoke rising from the hole left behind. The doctors said I was in shock and couldn't answer their questions, or wouldn't. What was I gonna tell them anyway? The truth? I thought it was best just to be quiet.

Since I was a kid the police released me to my parents. Mom and Dad's questions were harder to ignore. It was so hard to see my father crying and my mother pleading with me to tell them where Charles was.

The police said Charles had committed arson at the abandoned house and left me to "take the heat". They said he had become another of America's "missing youths". They figured he'd probably show up on the streets of the city one day and "then we'd be able to straighten this whole thing out". I think my parents want to believe that's all true. When I remembered my Dad's red eyes, I really understood his pain. My sister ... my brother ... God, I feel old.

So now here I am, sitting on Charles's bed, practicing flicking the blade of this knife. Mom is in bed with some pills the doctor gave her and Dad is in his den. I hear him sobbing and the clinking of yet another bottle as it is thrown away.

I've never felt more alone.

Earlier, I had wiped the blood from the knife's blade onto my shirt, but this time I washed the black stain on its blade with water out of a paper cup from my bathroom. I cried as I held the Bible and I prayed over that water, over that cup with the teddy bears dancing on its side. I don't know if it will pass as holy water, but I've heard love shall prevail. At least I hope so. I need to be strong.

I hear the back door; I think Charles just came home.

I love you, Charles.

Tick

The clock ticked. He was well aware of this, for his desk was placed below the maddening, mind-splitting incessant ticking. Colin looked up at the thing with bloodshot eyes. He figured he would get used to the persistent timepiece three years ago when he was first assigned this desk. Time was not his friend. He took the damned sound home with him. Went so far as removing all the batteries from his own clocks, just to find peace, some solitude. The only clock he had was a digital that had no tick, no sound at all. No sound at all. But yet he woke with the ticking in his ears every night. His upper lip curled slightly as he stared at this bane.

"Staring at the clock won't get your work done, Scard." Colin, jolted back into reality, turned to look at his supervisor. Bastard, what did he know about getting anything done but the new receptionist?

"Sorry, sir," Colin blurted, and turned back to his work. Mr. Johns seemed to be placated and moved on. Johns, a pudgy, slightly balding man lumbered toward his afternoon delight, the blonde of the month, leaving behind him a mixture of cologne and sweat. His cocky swagger seemed to prove it was good to be boss. Most eyes were trained on his back with disgust, and pity for his mousy little wife who was only seen at company functions. And the clock ticked.

Colin Scard had spent the last three of his 27 years of life at Jakes and Temple Inc., behind this same desk. Behind Trask, the same lard-ass college dropout, who had the tendency to scratch himself when no one was looking ... Well, no one but Colin. Colin had seen it all. The only thing that changed was the receptionists. Oh yes, they changed often too; seemed to be on the third one this year already. And it only being mid-February, Johns was tossing them quickly away before any "stink" could be made. But everything else stayed the same. The workload never seemed to thin. Colin felt lucky in this fact with the economy being in the toilet. It wasn't hard work either, mostly phone calls, straightening out some information that was unreadable or totally omitted from some application. The atmosphere was casual, as was the dress code. Asides from the receptionists, a person definitely didn't have to be attractive for their employment here. He was not a handsome man, nor hideous in that respect. But is a man defined by his looks? We like to scoff at this idea, but we find it true. We point and whisper, taking comfort in our own vanity. And how could it not shape a personality? Bringing out the darkness in one's heart, in one's soul. And the clock ticked.

Colin had not been sleeping well. Dreams. God-awful things. Not going to call them nightmares because most happened during his after-work naps. He couldn't stand to wake in total darkness after one of those dreams, so he attempted to stay awake the entire night. All he could ever recall was the rhythmic tapping behind his eyes. How his hands would reach up to press his eyeballs back into his skull. And how they seemed to pop like a couple of raw eggs in his hands. He woke in screams, covered with sweat and even soiled himself on a few occasions. At least when his eyes were open at home there was blessed quiet. Until he closed his eyes. And the clock ticked.

The red glow of the LED numbers illuminated the corner of his nightstand as he reached over to turn off the droning alarm. Colin sat up on the edge of the bed and looked at the empty side, almost expecting to hear Laura's soft breathing. Almost expecting to see her hair splayed out on the pillow. The sunlight filled the cracks around the room-darkening shade, invading Colin's sanctum. His stare transfixed on the unused side of the bed until the neighbor started his car. The bass of the teenager's car stereo reverberated through the apartment, breaking Colin's trance and filling his gut with a deep uneasiness. It had been another bad night of sleep. As the room first went silent last night, Colin discovered his new neighbors had put a clock on the wall, just on the other side of where he laid his head. The thin apartment walls echoed with the timepiece's progression. He had spent an hour rearranging his bedroom to get as far as possible from that wall, that sound. And the clock ticked.

Trask looked over his shoulder as Colin arrived. They exchanged informal nods before Trask turned back to his work. Colin settled at his desk and gave a quick glance at the clock. Trask quickly wheeled his chair close. "The word is, Johns got caught last night," Trask whispered. "His ol' lady went apeshit."

Neither this fact nor the lack of personal hygiene Trask emitted with every foul-smelling word surprised Colin. Did this man know his breath was deadly, or did he even care? Definitely was well-suited to work on the phone or maybe even radio, Colin mused. He fought back a chuckle, seeing Trask in a DJ booth. Scratching all night to the oldies. Colin turned and buried his face into his shoulder to escape the stench, or maybe just to stifle the laugh building inside. Trask looked at Colin for a reaction and was rewarded with a shrug.

"He's not in yet," the sewer on Trask's face continued. "Ya picked a good day to be late." The clock seemed extremely loud today, Colin thought as the last fume of Trask passed through his nose. "Could draw flies off fresh shit," his dad would say. Then it happened. Silence.

Colin had his eyes closed, fighting off a retch of

nausea when it occurred. His eyes flew open wide as he jumped up gaping at the clock. The judging eyes of his fellow employees fell upon him, already scheming up tales to be told at lunchtime. The clock had indeed stopped. The thing looked ... dead. Both hands hung straight down on the yellowing face. Colin knew clocks could stop. But this one had perished, it seemed, leaving this carcass of a timepiece with a thick layer of dust on its top and beautiful silence.

Trask tugged his sleeve and Colin turned his gaze to him. "What's up, dude?" the stench-hole implored. "You're freaking."

Colin smirked. What did this waste of a man know about freaking? It was like the burden of a lifetime was just lifted. He smiled wide and pointed at the clock, then opened his mouth to ... the clock ticked.

Eyes wide in disbelief and jaw agape, Colin stared. The clock continued its monotonous droning. Its arms at nine and two in a mocking half-smirk. The thing was far from dead; it actually looked new. Colin, with all eyes on him, sat down at his desk and vomited into his trash can. Oh yes, they have plenty of fodder for their lunchtime discussions today.

"Dude, maybe you should go home," Trask suggested. "Don't need that crap around here."

Colin didn't need to think this over long. He really needed to get out of there. He had just stood up to leave when Johns walked in. Johns seemed to survey the situation before he totally entered the office, looking like a fresh shower and a shave hadn't been on last night's agenda. His eyes settled on Colin.

"Going somewhere, Scard?" questioned Johns as he approached.

"Yes sir," Colin started as his eyes fell upon the scratches across Johns's face, "I'm really not feeling well." Then he noticed: Johns was blinking to the ticking of the clock; absolute synchronicity.

"If you have to go, I suppose," Johns stated as he looked into the trash can. "You'll need to work Saturday to catch up."

Colin would have agreed on giving up his firstborn to get out of there, away from that clock, away from his boss's blinking. It was insanity.

"Umm, Scard?" Colin turned; Johns was holding out the trash can. "Bring this back tomorrow, clean if you don't mind."

A slight giggle came from across the room. Colin accepted the receptacle and turned to leave. He glanced back in time to see Johns walking in the beat of the clock to his office. Colin felt his stomach begin to rise as he rushed into the men's room. He raised his head from the toilet when the door opened again. Trask entered, already unzipping his fly while walking to the urinal.

Colin did not intend to sleep today. He felt his heart race with the energy-drink triple-shot cocktail he had downed on the way home. *Damn foolish thing to do*, he thought, especially after hurling up his breakfast not more than a half hour ago. But his head throbbed and his ears seemed to play that awful ticking in his mind. He tried to convince himself it was the sound of his own heart; God knows, it sure was pumping hard. But that was it, the rhythm was wrong, no sync. Not like Johns. Colin supposed he could have put his hand on Johns' chest and felt his heart beat with the blinking of his eyes; with the ticking of the clock. The clock, that accursed clock. Colin had heard of people experiencing hallucinations after breathing in strong vapors or fumes, but if Trask's breath was that powerful, he should've had it tested by the FDA. Colin chuckled a little at this revelation. The clock had changed, he was sure of it. He pulled into the half-empty parking lot of his apartment and shifted his Volvo into park. He realized his shirt was covered in blood as he opened the car door.

Maria Cordova was concerned. The steady rapping on her door awoke her. She knocked over an empty water glass as she reached across her bedside table for her clock; *10:32* the red LED prominently displayed before her eyes. She had just worked an overnight shift in Borse County Hospital and it seemed to her that her head had just hit the pillow. The day-sleeper sign taped to her door had always given her the peace she needed. Until now. This sounded urgent. Feeling her nightshirt was modest enough, she quickly pulled on a pair of jogging shorts that were on top of a pile of laundry awaiting folding and headed down the hall. She cursed her decision as she noticed her nipples standing erect against the thin fabric of the shirt, but the knocking seemed lighter, weaker. She opened the door and her neighbor fell across her threshold. He was a bloody mess. That nice man who always seemed to help her with her trash. Who always had a smile for her. Who had been in a few fantasies in her quiet time with her vibrator. He needed her help, and fast. Mr. Scard seemed to be dying.

"A nose bleed?" Maria wondered out loud to herself. She was totally amazed at the amount of blood and the truly macabre mess he had made out of her front door. At the small puddle of blood that was coagulating on her front step. She had quickly assessed the situation and, with his head lying on the rolled-up rug from the entry, she ran to the bathroom for a cold washcloth. As she applied the compress to the bridge of his nose, his eyes looked into hers. It took her breath. She felt a deep-gut stirring, a tickling she wished would go away right now. At least for now.

"Sorry to bother you," Colin murmured. "I've made such a mess."

She smiled at him, still lying on the tile floor of her entry. The bleeding had stopped. "Hush now," Maria soothed as she felt his pulse. The corners of her mouth turned down as she felt his heart racing. He needed help. She went to the phone and dialed nine-one-one. The phone ticked in her ear. She looked at Colin, at those eyes. He looked back and their eyes locked in confusion as her bladder emptied and she fell, still holding the phone, into the puddle of her own urine. She attempted to diagnose the pain she felt as she fell, but was dead before her head bounced off the tile floor.

Wide-eyed, trying to process the horror playing out in front of his eyes, Colin screamed. It came out barely audible with a lack of breath. There she was, his neighbor, actually his savior, dead before him. Her eyes still staring at him, a somewhat accusatory stare. He attempted to stand and failed, falling to one knee on the tile floor. A jolt of pain coursed up his leg. Finally he was able to push his back against the wall and shove himself up. Then there it was ... coming from her; no wait, from the phone. Colin felt reality slipping as the phone ticked. Not only ticked but it seemed all the sounds of this apartment were starting to sync with it. Even the refrigerator seemed to drone in pulses. Colin's eyes darted across the room trying to rationalize it. Somehow. An illusion? A dream? His hand went to his chin and felt the dried blood crusted there begin to flake off in his grip. A torrent of tears began to etch a trail down his cheeks.

Darkness filled the edges of Colin's sight. Fear dried his eyes quickly as he reached for the doorknob. Turning to flee, he caught sight of a horrific image cast in the hallway mirror: a crimson mask with furrows cut down the cheeks, and familiar eyes. Colin stared in terror as the beast in bloodstained clothes stared back, mocking his fear, almost laughing it seemed. His hand, still on the knob, turned and pulled. Daylight poured onto his vision as he heard the stirring behind him. The sounds of the apartment were all one rhythmic pulse. Colin ran. Sanctuary of home was just three doors down. He hoped that would be far enough away from this madness, for now. It being midday allowed him to flee to his door unnoticed. He had tripped on the edge of the sidewalk and left an obscene smear of blood across the cement. As he stood, he found himself at his own door. He fumbled for his key with blood-caked fingers then escaped into the cool darkness, slamming the door.

The shirt felt like sandpaper on his chest with every gasp for breath. He gripped the edges and pulled hard as the buttons popped off, flying in several directions. One found its way to his aquarium, leaving a red trail, floating to the bottom. The fish nipped at it as it lay on a bed of blue rock. Colin peeled off the shirt, walking to the bathroom. Hands shaking, he turned on the water in the shower, left his clothes in a heap next to the commode and entered. The water left scarlet streaks to the drain as he let it cascade down upon his upturned face. After ten minutes and feeling weak, he sat on the floor of the tub. Pulling his knees to his face, he rolled into a fetal position. Colin closed his eyes and dreamed.

"C'mon baby," Laura's voice pleaded. With an outstretched hand she took his, pulling him close. Her needs, her love. She and Colin had met in high school and dated after Laura's boyfriend had an accident. A fatal accident. And now here she was, all his. Colin smiled as he fell on her, with a volley of lips and hands. She giggled at his inexperience, but he didn't mind. He'd have plenty of time to learn. Plenty of time to enjoy ... her. He closed his eyes and kissed her deeply, as the familiar smell of cologne and sweat filled his nostrils.

"What's the matter, Scard?" Johns said as Colin recoiled in horror. "Don't have time?" Johns, dressed in her nightie held him as the memory of Laura faded into Colin's screams and Johns's laughter.

Gasping and screaming, Colin awoke. The hot water was long gone, leaving a steady stream of cold pelting his body. His muscles were unresponsive at first, then he dragged himself over the side of the tub and rolled up into the bathmat. Reaching, pulling his terrycloth robe off its hook onto his shivering body, Colin screamed in anguish not only at the dream but the loss of Laura. Again. Anguish is the only true raw emotion.

Breath coming in hitches, Colin dressed quickly. He was being very mindful of every sound, every movement in his small apartment. People would be coming home soon and would follow the trail of gore to his front door. He peeked out the door as he opened it and walked briskly to his car. Took a quick glance at Maria's door and, astonishingly, the door was clean. Nothing looked out of place at all, except the red stain still ground into the cement by his door. "Doesn't matter," he mumbled to himself, then climbed into the Volvo and escaped. He drove two miles and stopped at the end of a grocery-store parking lot. Fighting back the tears for that long, he had reached his limitations. Soon he was sobbing.

"C'mon baby." Colin looked over and saw Laura through the fish-eyed lenses of his tears. He smiled at the dead woman.

"Get up lazy bones," Laura said with a smile. The two months since they married had been perfect. Colin reached up from the cocoon of sheets he had entwined himself in during the night and caressed her cheek. Her beautiful dark hair cascaded around his face as he received his morning reward of her soft lips. She giggled as she rose and Colin watched her in total awe of his fortune. "Going to the store to get some eggs for breakfast," she informed him. "Gotta feed my man so he can keep his strength UP."

Colin stretched open the front of his boxers and peeked in. "I don't know," he played. "Looking a little beat up."

Laura laughed and reached in the fly, and he found himself thinking about skipping breakfast. "I'll be right back." She jumped up. "Why don't you get a shower while I'm gone, and when I get back we'll scramble some eggs," she played as she patted his enlarging short fronts. Colin agreed, then she was gone. Forever is a long time to watch a clock waiting for someone to return.

Colin lifted his head from the front of the steering wheel, with a small string of mucus following behind. He looked over: Laura was not there. Laura was dead. Colin has identified her body at the morgue himself. A guard at a rest stop had found her car at the far end of the lot with a small pool of blood under the rear bumper. She had been beaten to death with a tire iron. Her face had been ... erased. She had only been gone two hours. The police ruled out robbery because her purse and jewelry were all untouched. The police had Colin in interrogation for only thirty minutes before they released him. Perhaps his grief was too much for the to bear watching any longer. *Random act of violence,* one detective had called it with a shrug of his shoulders. Not Laura, not her. Colin started the car and backed out.

The shadows from the rows of pines planted alongside the road gave a slow strobe effect to the interior of the car in the midday sun. Colin was unaware at first of the effect, was taken aback as he found himself mouthing a "tick" to each flash of daylight. His hands were only steadied by the wheel as he turned into the cemetery. Row 27, Plot 14. Laura was waiting, as she had been for six years. A small granite marker lay even with the grass displaying her name. His supposed future, his life was so empty. Time had no longer any meaning except the droning of the seconds. He stared down upon the gray stone, so polished he could see a distorted reflection of himself. In a moment of revelation, Colin smiled. Time was lonely. He laid the tire iron on the grave and walked back to his car. Time had come. He threw the trash can from the office onto the road as he drove away. The skin on the side of Trask's head peeled away as it bounced out from the can onto the unforgiving asphalt.

Karen Wilcox was having a bad day. Her alarm clock didn't go off, making her late for work. Of course it was not her fault; she couldn't have possibly turned it off in her sleep. As she ran out the door, her skirt got entangled on the branches of a bush jutting out into her sidewalk. And if that wasn't bad enough, someone had used the last of the morning caffeine at the office. She sent the secretary to the corner store to pick up a fresh bag of coffee. Karen hoped the woman had enough sense to get a decent brand after the realization she hadn't been specific to the lady. She was quite happy to stay busy so her mind didn't dwell on her personal problems. It was easier to listen to others' problems. Last night she had been surprised by the police looking for a patient of hers. They said Colin Scard had gone on a bit of a rampage. They wouldn't tell her anything else. He seemed like such an ordinary man. Had some problems with the loss of his wife, but that was to be expected. Certainly not the violent type.

She looked up as Colin entered her office.

"Mr. Scard, this is a surprise. Your appointment isn't until next week. Is there a problem? If you need to talk, I can open up some time after lunch." She looked behind him as he stood in the doorway, silently cursing the bad timing of running out of coffee. "My secretary just stepped out for a minute, but she'll be right back and we'll get you penciled in for later."

"Oh, she's back," Colin said as he tossed a small brick of coffee onto her desk. Its corner was crushed and had a few strands of hair that floated down behind it. Karen's eyes followed it down.

Cheap ass brand, oddly was her only thought, *Figures.*

Colin closed the door

"Does my time start now, Doc? Ya know, tick-tock. I locked the front door when I came in. I wouldn't want us to get cheated out of any ... time."

"Please sit down, Mr. Scard." She leaned forward on her desk to steady her legs; they felt almost like rubber. Her heart was pounding and her voice quavered. "Please?" Her eyes welled up with tears but he didn't seem to notice.

"Yeah," he stated as he sat down, "I could use a break."

Karen reached behind her and, finding the arms of her chair, lowered herself down onto it. She put her hands on the desk in front of her to try to stop them from trembling.

Colin brought his hands to his face and slid them back over his forehead, pushing his hair down. He puffed out his cheeks as he exhaled and looked at Karen. She thought about how exhausted he looked, but yet there was a spark in his eyes.

"How can I help you today, Mr. Scard?"

Colin's eyes were scanning the bookshelf behind her desk. It held several official-sounding books that Karen had picked up from the clearance bin at the local bookstore. She never opened them; strictly for ambiance. There was also an antique mantle clock that always needed to be wound. It stood silent, displaying 3:24 for about the last six months. His eyes rested on an object as he began to speak.

"I've been talking to my wife Laura." He spoke hesitantly.

"You do realize ..."

"Yes I realize! I know she's dead, I fucking killed her!" his voice boomed. "I killed her," he conceded in a whisper.

"Mr. Scard, I happen to know the pain you went through when she died. I refuse to believe that you murdered your wife. She was everything to you. I think you're just confused."

"She was going to see him! I couldn't allow that!"

"Who, Mr. Scard? Who was she going to see?"

"Benjamin Torres, that's who! Her old boyfriend. That same greasy son of a bitch that I had to ..."

Colin's eyes grew wide as they met Karen's gaze and he began to laugh in revelation.

"Oh shit!" he spoke between laughs. "Did I mess up!"

A thump outside the door was followed by a moan. Colin looked to the door and then back at Karen.

"Please, Mr. Scard, she might need help."

Colin smirked at her as he stood up and grabbed the brick of coffee again.

"Please!" Karen cried.

Colin went to the door and walked out. Karen quickly grabbed her cell phone and dialed nine-one-one before dropping it into her lap. There was a pounding on the other side of the door and Colin walked back in.

"Naw, she don't need any help, but I seem to have thrown coffee grounds all over your reception area. Put it on my bill," he sneered.

Karen tried to hold her composure; it was becoming increasingly more difficult. Colin sat in the chair facing the desk with his eyes focused at something on the shelf. Karen followed his gaze to the antique metronome being used as nothing more than a bookend.

"What is it, Mr. Scard? Would you like to see it?" Karen reached up and placed the musical timepiece on the desk in front of her. The phone on her lap slid down to the floor with a muffled thump. If it was heard he gave no sign, his attention totally on the wood-crafted box. She wanted to placate Colin any way possible to buy time. Karen wound the key on the side and released the pendulum.

The color drained from his face. He stared with his mouth agape. Tears flowed down Colin's cheeks and saliva etched a trail from the corners of his lips.

He looked up at Karen. "Make it stop," he pleaded in a hoarse whisper. She placed her hand on the pendulum and looked up at Colin.

He screamed in anguish, taking Karen by surprise. She snatched her hand back.

And the metronome ticked.

The parking lot for the office of Dr. Karen Wilcox soon was swarming with police vehicles. There was no sign of any distress from outside the building. The nine-one-one operator listened helplessly as the screaming started. It had been thirteen minutes since the call was placed. There had been dead air for the last six. A pair of officers with their guns drawn entered the reception area, sweeping their weapons to all corners of the room until they rested upon a prone figure that lay unmoving. The scent of fresh coffee filled the air.

Why's this happening? Colin beat his hand on the steering wheel. *The Doc was supposed to help me. She's just one of them. Burning into my mind with that sound, that pulse. It splits my head open. Is there no rest?* Colin was deep in thought as the car behind him honked its horn. The light had changed. He gave a wave over behind himself and drove through the intersection. Colin looked into the rearview mirror at Laura in the backseat; she was laughing.

"Tick, Tick, you're just a bomb!" Laura spoke from the rear. "C'mon baby, lets blow!"

"But baby," he spoke to the empty mirror, "what happened?" He was answered with silence; blessed silence.

The man in the car behind Colin watched him drive away and gasped as he saw the object dragging behind tied to the bumper – then started to laugh. Damn, that mannequin looked real, he mused. These college boys are always pulling some crazy pranks.

Colin drove around the back roads near the old rock quarry for twenty minutes and discovered there wasn't much left on the rope to discard into the pit of aqua-blue. He looked up at the sun and wiped a tendril of sweat from his brow before bending over to complete his task .Colin noticed how ragged and gnawed her fingernails looked and smirked at the thought of the Doc chewing her nails. He untied the hand and flipped it over his shoulder; listened to it splash lightly in the water. A cloud of white dust was all he left behind as he drove away. A couple miles down the road, Colin saw the head lying on the trail and felt the satisfying 'POP'as his wheel shot brains into the nearby foliage. He looked into his mirror and saw how happy Laura was and knew it was a good day.

The sun had awakened Libby Maxwell as it beamed into her window at daybreak. She felt that was the proper way to get up in the morning. Whereas others dreaded arising, Libby wanted to face the day with both feet on the ground. She enjoyed her independence after a failed marriage. It wasn't either one's fault, they were oil and water, fire and ice; found out a little late they just didn't mesh. Libby didn't mind living alone. She had no one to answer to; that suited her just fine. After a splash of cold water on her face, Libby began her daily regimen of a five-mile jog. The back roads were the best place to run. One could enjoy a small slice of nature without becoming road pizza by the more-than-numerous rock trucks that barreled along the main roads. She made it a habit to stop in the little convenience store at the edge of the highway before turning back toward home. The place was owned by two older men, who scrabbled to the counter every morning when she came in. They made sure to have a bottle of water set out for her in the front cooler, so they would have more time to chat to the beautiful woman with the infectious smile. She would then stroll back leisurely to admire the color of the leaves, or the sound of the birds. She truly enjoyed her independence.

She was a half mile from the car when she spotted it parked on the side of the road. It hadn't been there thirty minutes ago when she ran down the road. *Has to be lost,* she thought. *Yep, definitely lost.* Nearing the car, she could see a man bent over the back fender changing the tire. Libby coughed lightly approaching the man, so as not to startle him.

"Seems you are not having the best of luck today," she casually sympathized. The man obviously knew nothing about changing a tire. He was clad in a dark T-shirt and the sun was intense on his back. The narrow strip of skin above his collar was a nasty shade of pink. Libby knew he'd feel that later. The man glanced up with irritation in his eye, which seemed to soften as he saw her face.

"Can't seem to get a signal on my cell," he griped as he wiped the sweat from his face.

"Nope, not out here you won't." Libby smirked. "But I can tell you what to do, if you provide the muscle. First, I think you could use this more than me at the moment." She held her bottle of water to him. "Don't worry, I'm pretty sure I was cleared of cooties last week."

He gave a light chuckle and accepted the water, twisting off the cap and taking no time in draining the plastic bottle. "Thank you. My name's Colin, and I am proud to meet you," he added with a sincere smile.

"Well, I'm Libby and let's get that tire changed before you call me a hero."

Colin had listened to her instructions, and soon the car was on four tires again. He stood up, brushing the dust from his knees. "I can't thank you enough. I'm just trying to get home to my wife. I guess I took a wrong turn and got lost."

"I figured as much," she chuckled. "Nobody comes out here unless they lose their way."

"And you?" Colin implored. "You lost too?"

Libby treated him with that infectious smile. "Naw, I live around the corner."

"Do you think I could impose on you for a favor? I really need to use a restroom."

"Hmmm," she played, inspecting him for a moment with a chuckle, "you're not a killer, are you?"

"No, just lost my way." His tone was soft as he watched Laura smile from the backseat of the car.

Libby guided Colin to her house from the passenger seat. He spoke of his wife and how good it would be to get home to her. They were less than a mile from their destination, and Colin did seem more than anxious to get there.

"So where is home?" she questioned, as she opened her front door.

Colin smiled, too big. Libby felt the color drain from her face.

"Right here, you little bitch."

She tried to push the door closed, but he pushed back harder.

Libby screamed and backed into the living room, as Colin approached. Suddenly he stopped and looked around. Falling to his knees, his hands went to his ears. The walls were covered with clocks. The golden pendulums swayed, filling the room with the resounding thunder of the timepieces. He wept loudly, feeling the beats in his heart syncing with the ticking. The maddening sound telegraphed though his body. Every muscle twitched with the rhythmic passing of time. The blood pumping through his hands played the sounds right to his ears. He stared at Libby, as she ran out past him. Unable to move, with his mouth agape and drooling, paralyzed with fear, in the workshop of *Libby's Clock Repairs.*

Libby raced the five miles back to the store, watching over her shoulder for Colin to be chasing behind her; it was unnecessary. The police found him still in the room, unresponsive. He had pissed his pants.

Colin lay on the table with his limbs strapped down. He looked across the room to the glass wall at the faces of strangers who had come to witness this spectacle. Laura sat on the front row. He watched her as they stuck the needles in his arm.

"C'mon baby," she mouthed, then her face melted into a raw pulp with a jagged section of her skull jutting out from the gore. "I'm waiting for you." Then she was gone.

"I'm sorry," Colin whispered.

He turned his gaze toward the large clock face as the second hand snapped away the seconds.

Five seconds till midnight.

And the clock ticked.

Wind-Borne

The wind whispered through the long grasses.
Frank lay on his belly as car headlights passed. A
spotlight lit up the ground near him. The breeze blew
harder and the grass hissed a tune as it danced above
his head. The car moved on. Frank looked up and saw
the light-bar on the vehicle in the distance. Cursing
himself for wandering out into a field where there was
no cover, no place to hide, he looked skyward. The
shadows of the clouds playing off the ebbing sun cast a
slight yellowish hue to the grayness of the oncoming
night.

He'd been lucky this time.

Only if that old bastard had just given him his
money, but he felt the need to be a tough guy and fight.
Frank had to stick him with the knife. The only thing
his father ever gave him had been a few broken ribs and
that knife. Now he used it to get a little bit of cash to
wash away his problems with a twelve-pack of beer. It
had worked well until this feeble old man decided to
become a hero to his wallet and got six inches of steel in
his gut for the trouble. Frank could still feel the hot
blood spurt out onto his hand. He was still staring at
the knife when a lady screamed.

Frank ran.

The clouds raced across the sky on a trek carried
by the strong winds that had been building. Frank put
his back to the breeze and followed the course of
Nature's breath. The squall of air pushed him onward,
howling in his ears. Then the wind stopped abruptly. He
raised his eyes. A half moon silhouetted a large figure

before him.

"Oh my God," Frank muttered.

The figure chuckled and then spoke. Each word seemed to be carried upon a gust of air. "Pray to your deity if you must. It will be unanswered. There are no gods or demons, although that does not mean evil doesn't exist." Its breath blew across Frank's face with the stench of the grave. "It is scattered on the earth waiting for some luckless bastard to stumble upon it to do its bidding." The words echoed in the moving air.

Frank drew his father's blade once again. With shaking hands he lashed out at the figure. The knife met no resistance.

A small whirlwind began at Frank's feet. He screamed as he felt it using the grasses to tear away his clothes, then his skin. The air shrieked with him in a horrific chorus.

"But there are times when the wind collects the evil from the area, and it howls as it gains form ..."

Standing with knife in hand, Frank's lips parted in a deep exhale. When his ankles gave way, he fell as the figure embraced him.

"...and becomes pure Hell on earth." The words trailed off in the night breeze.

Christmas Spirit

Chad was alive: to begin with. The eggnog was poured and the mistletoe hung in a strategic place. He looked around at his house quite pleased at himself with his decorating prowess. Humming a little Christmas tune along with the single speaker that housed his IPod. It was loaded with holiday songs for this joyous night. Chad smiled as he imagined Kate's face when she entered the room and spied the small box hung by a beautiful gold ribbon on the front of the grand tree. The tree had to be wonderful; actually everything had to be wonderful on this night. He had played this night in his mind for weeks: she would open the box and see the ring. She would say yes and hug him tightly as her lips touched his. The taste of her cherry lip-gloss, the slight scent of her perfume, he had imagined it all. He stood in front of the hallway mirror and adjusted the line of bells adorning his lapel with a twinkle in his eye when the doorbell chimed. He giggled with glee as he opened the door in anticipation of the night ... no ... the life to come.

A child was huddled shivering against the door. The snow collected in her golden hair, melting into translucent strings. As the light from the room found its way into her upturned eyes, Chad swore she glowed. The icy blue stare from her eyes brought a chill down Chad's spine.

"Hey little one, what's your name? What are you doing out on a night like this? For heaven's sake, where is your mother?"

The girl did not reply, just a cold stare from her

blue eyes. Chad reached for a decorative blanket of a pastoral winter scene from the top of the sofa and wrapped it around the small frame of the child. He winced at the bitter cold as he closed the door. She was not dressed for the weather, and Chad was truly concerned as the back of his hand brushed the girl's cheek — it had no warmth.

"There shall be visitors, there shall be three," she whispered in a breath that floated in the air like the night's frost.

"Let's get you warmed up, before you catch your death of cold." He led her to the hearth where a small fire was slowly consuming a few split pieces of oak as he went after the phone. Chad looked over to her as he pressed a second number one on the keypad and stopped. The blanket lay in a pile on the hearth. Walking to it as he held the phone, the legs of a white rabbit kicked out in spasms. Its entrails had been pulled into the blanket and a number three was written in blood on the white marble hearth. The child was gone.

"Nine-One-One Emergency," the phone droned in his ear, "what is the nature of your emergency?"

Chad stood transfixed at the bloody mess on his fireplace, trying to sort things in his mind.

"Hello?" The voice called out again. "We will be sending an officer to your location."

"No, no." Chad found his voice. "There has been a mistake." And pushed the end button on the phone. He knelt down to study the spot as the rabbit and the number melted away into stone, leaving only the blanket on a blank slate of marble. Stomach churning, he steadied himself. Perhaps a bit of undigested beef? he thought. But in his heart he knew there was more grave to this than gravy. Three, she said. *No, not tonight,* he pondered. *I'd rather not.*

He was contemplating what had happened as a

rapping came to the door. Chad stood as the hall clock began its Westminster chimes to announce ten in the evening, too early to be Kate.

The rapping grew impatient.

"Chad? ... Chadster?" a young man's voice queried.

"No, it can't be. " Hesitantly, Chad opened the door.

Eddie Cleave stood in the doorway with a cocky smirk. His face untouched by the dozen years since Chad had seen him last, since anyone had seen him last. Eddie was dead.

"Hey, hey, Chadster!" Eddie pushed his way in through the doorway. "Long time no see!" he added with a punch to the arm. The bells on Chad's lapel jingled with the blow.

"I don't understand, Eddie, you're ..."

"I'm what, Chadster? Go ahead and spit it out. Spill the beans. Tell me! I'm dead? Don't ya think I know that? And here I am spending a sparse few moments back on terra firma with an asshole that has the uncanny ability to spout the fuckin' obvious." With a grin, Eddie continued: "Just messing with ya, Chaddy boy, but I have some special friends who wanted me to show you some things. So c'mon now and let's get a move on." Then Eddie's face went solemn. "We don't have all night."

"I don't understand!" protested Chad. "I can't go anywhere, I have company coming, and I'm not dressed for the night."

With a chilling stare, Eddie whispered while gripping Chad's arm, "You won't feel a thing."

The walls evaporated into a misty fog, and Chad's eyes focused on a figure bent over a huddled form in a corner of the room. The smell of a burnt dinner filled the air. Chad remembered this scene often with his father and mother.

"Ya burnt the damn turkey, didn't ya, bitch? Why the hell do I continue hoping things will change around here?"

"Please! Please, Henry! I'm so sorry!" she blubbered, holding her hands up to protect her face from any more blows. Chad had seen the fear in her one eye that wasn't swollen shut.

"And that boy of yours! Little faggot! Son of a bitch doesn't even know how to throw a ball, and where the hell is Shelly? Probably out whoring around again. Bitch gonna come home pregnant, mark my words."

"Daddy?"

All eyes in the room turned to look at a seven-year-old boy standing in the doorway, wearing a face Chad had seen in many mirrors over the years.

"Now, you go back to watching television, Chad, you're mothers got some more learning to do."

The boy stared at his mother.

"Now go, Goddammit, before I tell Santa not to come tonight!"

Chad could tell the boy's eyes were full of tears because his were too.

"C'mon Chad," Eddie prodded, "we need to go."

As the room faded away, Chad could still hear sounds of his mother's cries as his father beat her.

Chad wiped his tears as the room filled his view. A teenage girl sat on a table digging in her purse. Chad watched as his sister Shelly counted out money into the hand of an old woman, who spirited it away quite ungracefully.

"Now, remove your panties and lie down, dear. I'll be right back. It won't take long, so you can get home to your family for Christmas." The old lady sneered with a mouthful of blackened stumps, bringing Chad into awareness of what was about to happen. With a lump in his throat, he turned to Eddie.

"Take me away! Please, I don't want to see this."

Eddie took pity on him and grabbed his arm as the old woman passed between them with a wire in her hand.

Chad closed his eyes.

Bong, the hallway clock reported. Chad opened his eyes and looked up at the timepiece and was in sudden realization that he was alone again and he had returned before the tenth strike. With weak knees he collapsed on the sofa and lowered his head into his hands. He had spent many years trying to forget, and it had hit him back hard.

"No!" he exclaimed aloud. "I'm not going to let this destroy all I worked for. I've grown past all that." He stood up and walked to the mirror and stared into his own face. The thought of Kate flowed through his mind and brought a twinkle back into his eyes. The room filled with the sound of a truly beautiful version of "Oh Holy Night". He smiled and thought of his sister Shelly and how he needed to find her again. Bring her back into his life. Everybody deserved to feel the love and joy the holiday brought him.

Then the music stopped.

Chad turned around quickly as an obese man sitting in a lawn chair began to laugh behind him. Clad in Bermuda shorts and a stretched tank top that Chad guessed used to be white but now was a conglomerate of stains, the man stopped laughing and seemed to be concentrating.

"Who are you?" Chad's eyes widened in surprise.

"Hold on a second," the stranger implored as he leaned to the side and passed gas loudly then settled back down. The chair creaked under his weight as the stench spread and made Chad retch.

"Who I am is not important. What I show you will be."

"Forget it; I don't need your poison. Can't you see

I'm expecting a visitor? Now, be off with you before I call the police!"

This brought a roll of laughter from the man who began to cough and spit up a large ball of phlegm onto Chad's floor. In an almost impossible speed, the man leapt up and grabbed Chad's arm.

"Shut up and come with me, you fuck."

An odor of urine also came as the room focused in Chad's eyes. A gaunt figure sat on a stained mattress with a glass tube and a lighter. Immediately Chad knew it was Shelly. The beautiful woman he once knew was no longer in control of her own life. A toilet flushed and a black man came back into the room.

"You need to wash yo ass, bitch. Ain't nobody gonna pay for that pussy all stinkin'. After ya finish that rock, I want ya ta get back out on the street."

"But it's Christmas Eve!" Shelly whined. "Let me just enjoy my present."

"Yer gonna just sit and smoke it all up at once, ya stupid bitch."

Chad's heart sank watching his sister, wishing there was something he could do. The fat man beside him began to chuckle.

"Don't worry about her," the rotund spirit snickered, "doesn't she look happy?"

Chad looked back at his sister as she took a draw off her pipe then closed her eyes in ecstasy.

"She'll stop doing drugs tonight. A couple college kids decide that she wasn't worth the money they had paid her and then ..."

"What do you mean?"

"You figure it out, Einstein. C'mon, time to go."

"I don't want to see any more."

The obese man smiled.

"You'll wanna see this, trust me."

"But why me?"

The big man grinned.

"Why not you? You just seemed too happy."

A dim hallway surrounded them as their surroundings came into view. The sound of lovemaking came from behind a door.

"Why did you bring me here? What could this possibly have to do with me?"

"Shhhh, listen ..." The fat bastard put his hand to his ear in a mock show of concentration in listening.

Chad's face drew ashen as he recognized the moaning female voice.

"Kate might be late tonight." The man laughed until his face turned red and he began coughing.

Chad fell to his knees and sobbed as the couple reached orgasm.

The fat man put his hand on Chad's back. "Merry Christmas, ya dumbass."

A knock on his door made Chad look up and realize he was back home. With his breath hitching, he looked around the room with different eyes. All the bright decorations had no place in this cold dim world. The knocking behind him made him stare at the door.

"Who the hell is it?" Chad yelled out. "You made your point. I don't need to see more to tell me this world is full of garbage."

"Police, sir. Open the door, please."

"What do you want?"

"We received a nine-one-one call from this location, and I have to check things out. Now open the door, sir."

Chad took off the jacket with the bells on the lapel and threw it into a corner with disgust. He tried to maintain a degree of composure walking to the door and opened it. A cold blast of air slapped him in the face as the uniformed man stepped into the foyer.

"Did you make the call, sir?"

"Yes sir, I'm really sorry, I'm having a really bad night. I misdialed. Now, if there's nothing else ..."

The officer grabbed Chad's arm.

"Oh, why so fast, sir? We have somewhere to go."

Chad tried to pull back but the officer held him in a death grip.

"Oh, you're one of them. I don't know what you want; you've already messed up my life. I mean, what the hell is left?"

"No sir, we did nothing but point things out to you. Your life was already messed up. You were just too stupid to realize it."

Chad stared at the officer. "OK, let's go. I grow tired of these games."

"We are already here."

Chad looked around; nothing had changed.

"What do you mean? We didn't go anywhere."

"Look under the tree."

The ribbon that once held a golden box onto the tree was now wrapped around the slender neck of Kate. Her eyes were blood-red and she was lying in a pool of her own urine.

"Are these visions of what will be? Or just may be?" Chad whispered with a heavy heart.

The officer said nothing, he just pointed into the bedroom. In the gloom Chad could see an unmoving crumpled heap on the floor, a pistol beside the body. The slight scent of sulfur drifted in the air.

"What do you want from me?"

A dark grin spread across the officer's face. "Thought you'd never ask."

"Daddy, wake up! Daddy!"

Chad sat up on his bed to look into the face of a little blonde-haired girl with large blue eyes.

"Daddy, come on! Let's open the presents! Mommy said to get you!" She giggled before running out of the room in her white rabbit slippers.

Chad smiled while rubbing his eyes.

Yeah, it was worth a soul.

Flesh& Blood

I watched as Tipper died. We called the dog that due to its solid coat of white fur with a black tip on its tail. Now a crimson stain covered the large canine's pelt. It hadn't been a clean shot, and the dog almost screamed before it fell and writhed on the floor of the barn. The chain that bound Tipper to the post dragged behind, clinking out the spasms with a metallic sound. The dog's muzzle left a trail of foaming drool on the dark floorboards. My twelve-year-old fingers still wrapped around the trigger of the rifle. Pa put his hand on my back as I fought the tears. He reached across my shoulder and took the weapon of wood and steel. It didn't seem to take the weight off my heart. He cocked the firearm and quickly shot Tipper in the head. The dog's agony was over. I could no longer hold back the pain I felt, the anguish a boy shouldn't have to deal with. I'd rather die than to suffer that feeling again.

Rather die.

"It hadda be done, boy."

I looked up at Pa's weathered face. His soft blue eyes seemed so out of place under his heavy brow. The creases in his skin looked deeper than I had ever remembered them. I think we both aged a few years on that day. I knew he was right. Tipper had gone rabid. We had chained him inside the barn the day after he was bit. Pa said it was probably a coon or a possum that got him. There were always a few sick animals wandering around the fields at night. But we hadn't known for sure, so we chained him. I fed and made sure he had water for pretty near two months. He had howled every night. Just lonesome, I 'spect. I would go in and ruffle the fur on the top of his head. The dog's tail wagged so fast it was a blur. Pa had gotten so angry when he saw that I was within the boundary of the chain. He yelled so loud then grabbed me in a hug. He was shaking. I tried to tell him Tipper was fine and we could let him go, but he said it was still too early.

The dog started getting sick. I hadn't told my father at first. I mean, maybe it just had a cold from sleeping in this barn instead of the rug at the foot of my bed. I told myself that for two days until the dog went mad. Jumping and testing the strength of the chain as I entered. I stood in the doorway while my pet growled and snapped at the air, slinging frothy spittle. I went to the house and got Pa. He grabbed his rifle and walked back down to the barn with me. When we got to the door he handed me the weapon. I looked up at him with shocked eyes.

"Gotta take care of your own, boy."

"But ..." Once I saw his face, I knew there was no need in arguing. It was my dog, my burden.

He helped me bury Tipper after a short respectful moment. We dug the hole together, and after he hauled the dog into it he walked away. I'm glad he did. I didn't want him to see the weakness that still resided in my youth, the pain in my heart. When I finished filling the grave, I went into the barn. Pa was hosing away the blood and the dog's wastes from the night. Daylight filled all but the darkest corners of the barn. The horse tromped around in its stall as I passed. Pa looked up.

"Come here, boy, and rinse your face. Then tend to the horse. Life goes on, remember that."

Yeah, life goes on.

We lost my mother a few months later. She was never a large woman but always handled her share of the work. A hot breakfast and a good dinner were a necessity when working on a farm. And after my chores, she would drive me into town for school singing to the radio. I hadn't heard some of the songs before, but it always made me feel good. Sometimes at home, Mom would play the radio loud and dance while doin' her housework. She dropped me off one day and a rock truck silenced her songs forever. No one picked me up that day. I walked the seven miles to the farm. Pa was working in the field, and I looked for Mom. He finished the acre he was in and parked the tractor in the shade of the barn. Then he rinsed his face. Funny, I had never seen him do that before. Funny ... life goes on.

We managed the fall harvest that year. I had to drop out of school until harvest ended. I could make it up over summer. There were a few families like that around here. Farms were hit hard durin' this recession thing I'd heard about. We had a few field hands but couldn't afford to keep them year-round, so Pa relied on me more to help fill the spot Mom left. My cooking skills weren't the best, yet my father never complained. Having cleaned up the dishes, we'd sit at the table and play cards. Mostly we talked. A man had plenty of time to think while working the fields every day. The droning of the engine would be forgotten, and Pa said it was like his body goin' on auto-pilot as his mind took him away. He often spoke of his hopes and fears while dealing the cards. I'd listen and daydream of being someplace other than the farm.

Dreams came hard on a farm. The future wasn't pretty because farms were handed down to the sons. So basically, this was what I had to look forward to. Dirt and seed. It was a necessary position to fill for the country's needs. But not for mine. I saw the jets stream across the skies, leaving tracks of white in their paths. *National Geographic Magazine* once had a bird's-eye-view of farmland. The green rows checker-boarded across the hills. You could even see a tractor plowing up some land in the distance. That's what it looked like from up there; down here it was just dirt and seed.

Mr. Morsly was in the field this morning.

He was our closest neighbor, and yet he still lived a mile or so away. I'd often gotten a ride from school with him if he passed me walking home. Dad would always take me to school after my chores, but it was up to me to get back. So whenever I saw that old white pickup with the Morsly Farm magnet hanging from the driver's door, I was relieved. He'd have the radio belting out some twangy country music, and a line of tobacco juice running down the creases of his mouth. The truck stank like beer and man-sweat, but it was much finer than the long walk home. He had a son who still lived with him. Pa said he was slow. I didn't understand what that meant. Heck, Mike Morsly was pretty near thirty and could run like the wind. He just liked to play games and laugh. When I got a pocketknife for Christmas last year, I taught Mike how to play mumblypeg. It was fun till he threw the blade into my foot. I limped around a couple weeks but I never told. They woulda sure taken away my knife, and he didn't mean to do it. When Mom died, I found a pickle jar full of wildflowers on the porch. The flowers were half-dead and their stems were broken. But they were beautiful. Though Mike wasn't the smartest fellow in the world, he sure was thoughtful.

I was coming out of the chicken coop with some eggs for our breakfast and looked across the horizon. The solid line of the distant land was interrupted by a single figure. I could tell by the man's walk it was Mr. Morsly. I could also tell he was naked.

I ran over to my father and told him. He was hand-pumping fuel into the tractor. "Topping 'er off" to finish the job, he traversed the yard wiping his hands on a rag. He studied the sight for a moment. Mr. Morsly was still on his ambling trek across the field.

"What's the matter with him, Pa?"

"You go in and get your breakfast. I'll be back to take you to school. Looks like Morsly might need a hand." He went into the barn and grabbed a horse blanket. Even in the company of men, a fellow deserved some dignity. The flatbed truck, still half loaded with hay bales, sat in front of the barn. I often drove it around the farm to help out. The driver's door squealed as Pa got in. A gun rack in the back window held a shotgun. I had only fired it once to kill a rattlesnake, and it gave me quite a bruise on my shoulder. But on the farm a feller needed to be ready for anything. There was all kind of dangerous stuff. Swinging the gate for my father to drive through, I watched a trail of dust behind the truck as it crossed the field before I entered the house. Gazing back, I saw him stop near the man, then I closed the door.

There were a few slices of ham from the previous night wrapped in plastic inside the fridge. I was throwing them on some bread when I heard the distinctive sound of a shotgun. The noise drifted over the field. Dropping the sandwich, I turned towards the door just as Mike Morsly came in.

"Hey, Mike, you know you're supposed to knock ..."

The man was hurt. Actually, I didn't know how he was standing. His throat was ripped out, leaving ragged flaps of skin that swayed as he moved. My eyes grew wide in disbelief. His breathing whistled from the hole in his neck.

"Mike? Cripes, Mike!"

He looked at me with eyes that held no recognition. A graying face, and lips the color of coal peeled back to almost perfect teeth. He grunted, the sound making a spray of blood and spit fly from his wound. Then he leapt towards me, only to be stopped by the kitchen table that groaned against the floor under his weight. I backed up to the stove, and I ain't ashamed to say I pissed my pants slightly. The tears flowed from my eyes as I saw my friend push himself up from the table and, in almost an afterthought, look at me. Mike never took his eyes off me, continuing to walk, the table between us scraping strides across the wood floor. I searched a nearby drawer until I found the biggest knife and held it out in front of me. The blade shook in fear as I tried to control my hand. A long line of drool dribbled from his dark lips onto his chin as he pushed against the far side of the table. I stabbed at his hands as they came into reach of his outstretched arms. Even though the blade ripped into his hands and arms, he didn't seem to care.

The air exploded in a wave of sound and blood; Mike's head disappeared. Pa was at the doorway, lowering the shotgun from his shoulder. Mike fell, his arms slapping the top of the table before following the rest of his body to the floor. I looked down at my blood-covered arms and dropped the knife. Descending from my hand, the blade balanced on its tip before clattering into the spreading blood on the table. I ran to my father.

His shirt was torn, and I could see his chest rise and fall as he fought to catch his breath. The shotgun in his left hand, he pulled me close with his right and hugged me. The bottoms of his jeans were soaked in blood.

"Did he hurt you, boy?" Pa asked, giving me a look-over.

"No." I lifted my face to his. "Why'd he do that? He was my friend."

"Dunno, his father was the same way. Attacked me soon as I got out of the truck. He was messed up, messed up real bad." Exhaling sharply through his nose, my father's hand shook as he brought it up to his face and wiped his brow. "I climbed back in the truck, but he wasn't right in the head and kept pounding and snappin' his teeth at me from the other side of the glass."

"Do ya think it's rabies? Clive Kinson at school said there's been a lot of it goin' round again."

"Hmmm." My father considered for a moment. "I don't think so. Just saw him last week and he was fine. Rabies doesn't change a man that quick. Run out to the barn and get one of those tarps. I'm gonna call the Sheriff."

I nodded and turned towards the door.

"Jessie?" My father stopped me. "Here, take this with." He handed me the shotgun. The weight of the weapon seemed to have doubled since I used it to shoot the snake. Sure felt like it. "Be careful." I walked to the door and stopped. Through the screen came the smells of the farm. Wind blew a small dust devil in front of the barn, which spun away quickly to the field.

"You think there's others, Pa?"

"I dunno. Now, you run along and fetch that tarp."

Stepping out into the yard, I was aware of every movement, every sound. I stopped and listened; the breeze cut across the plowed acres without anything to stop it. It echoed in my ears. The chickens continued their noisy squabbles over food, and the horse snorted his dislike for being so late in the stall. Yeah, everything seemed so ordinary. I shifted the gun in my hands and went to the barn. The smell of fresh hay hung in the air heavily. I went to the rear shelves where we stored the supplies and found an old blue tarp stacked on a pile of silver ones sealed in packages. I tucked it under my arm and swiveled to leave, until my eyes rested on the chain that was still attached to the post. It had been pretty near a year, but I couldn't take it off.

When I returned to the house, Pa was hanging up the phone. Clearing his throat, his eyes met mine. I could tell he didn't like what he had heard. I handed him the tarp and without a word, we rolled Mike's body into it.

"When is he coming?" I broke the silence.

"He isn't. Now grab that end." Pa motioned with his head to the other side of the tarp. I walked to the opposite side of the roll, happy I didn't have to lift the other, which was now sitting in a small pool of blood. I picked it up by the ends of the tarp and helped my father lug it to the truck.

"Why's he not coming?" I was puzzled. Here there were two dead bodies, and the Sheriff wasn't interested? That just didn't make sense.

"Never talked to him." Pa exhaled and leaned on the tailgate of the truck. "Somebody else answered the phone, I don't know who. The fellow wasn't talking right. There was screaming and yelling in the background. Then he said 'Everything's gone!' and hung up."

I watched my father's shoulders slump a little that day. I had never seen it before. He was unsure what to do next. He stared at the ground for a bit and opened his mouth to speak, thought for a second, then shut it again.

"So what we gonna do, Pa?"

He seemed to ponder the question then sighed. "I don't know."

"What about Sarah? I hope she's alright."

My father glanced down at me with realization in his eyes. "Go to the truck," he said. "Bring the shotgun."

Sarah was Mr. Morsly's niece. She had a little trouble with her parents and they sent her to help out with Mike. I'd never seen a girl with so many tattoos. I guess those city girls are a bit different than the ones around here. But she sure was pretty. When she looked at me with her green eyes, I had a funny feeling in my gut, kinda like when you drive over a hill real fast. Yeah, I was definitely sweet on her. She was the only one who ever made me feel like when Mike had shown me one of Mr. Morsly's magazines. The lady in it was naked and stretched out on a bed. I got to inspect it only a minute until we were caught. I went home that day quickly, while Mike got yelled at.

Pa drove fast to the Morsly farm. Nothing seemed unusual except that the door stood wide open. Long tracks of blood streaked down the white paint, like someone was trying to get in. Appeared they did, too. Skip, Mike's black lab, lay in the dust of the driveway. The dog's side was ripped open to the bone. A swarm of flies flew up into a small cloud as my father stopped the truck, before settling back down on the carcass.

"You wait here." He regarded me sternly. "If anyone, and I mean anyone, comes and tries to get inside the truck, you shoot them. You hear, boy?"

"But Pa ..."

"Hush now, and lock the doors. I'll be right back." He got out, watched me secure the locks, and walked slowly toward the Morsly house. I surveyed the yard. It coulda been any other day. Nothing was different, nothing at all. My father stood on the porch peering into the doorway, and then he went in.

A light breeze blew across the tops of the field in waves. The earth could dance better than Fred Astaire sometimes. The wind twisted and turned the fresh grasses in wondrous patterns. I would sit at my window as storms blew in and watch nature showing me how powerful my world really was. The glass rattling in its frame protecting me from the moving air outside. But it had never felt this small before. So ... insignificant.

I pressed my nose against the glass of the door and peered into the gloom of the Morsly's house. After a few minutes my father reappeared in the entryway and motioned for me to come. I climbed out and stepped on the dirt of the driveway. Reaching into the truck, I grabbed the shotgun by the stock and carried it to the house like Pa had shown me. By your side and barrel up, he'd always said, and there will be no accidents. The porch steps were red with blood.

"She in there, Pa?"

"I think so. Got herself all locked up in a bathroom, and she won't open the door. Maybe you can talk to her, get her to unlock it."

"Okay, I'll try."

"Before we go in, there's a body in the living room. Don't look if you can help it, he's pretty torn up. I think it's Beau Grant from up the road. Just keep walking with your eyes straight. He can't hurt you."

I followed my father inside where the gloom attacked me, and squinted to make out the shapes of the furniture in the foyer. The antique grandfather clock in the living room chimed the hour, filling the house with sound; it seemed so normal. As my eyes adjusted, I seen Mike's trail boots placed carefully together at the door. He was so proud of those boots when he got them for his birthday last week. Now they stood waiting for feet that would never jump or run in them again.

"C'mon, boy, I don't want to be in here any longer than necessary."

I did as I was told and didn't even look into the living room as we passed. I must admit the room had a smell to it. Not real strong, but I didn't want to remember it. When we got to the bathroom door, I could see the dark stains of blood down its front. They had tried to get in here too, but this door stayed shut. I could hear her weeping and tapped on the wood with my knuckles, mindful not to touch the blood.

"Sarah?" There was no response but crying. "Sarah, it's Jessie from down the road. You know, Mike's friend." In the back of my mind I could still see his hand slapping the table as he fell.

"Mike's dead!" she screamed out from behind the door. I looked at Pa. I mean, how could she know that? "Go away! Leave me alone!"

"I wish you'd come out here so we could make sure you're all right. If you want, you can go back in there afterwards. There's nobody here but me and my dad. Please?"

"It hurts."

Dad stepped forward. "What hurts, Sarah?"

"My arm where Mr. Grant bit me. Why'd he do that? Creepy old dude. Mike grabbed him, and they were wrestling and then ..." She started sobbing real loud. "And then he ripped out Mike's throat with his teeth!"

The door opened and she ran into my father's arms. It looked funny to watch him calming her down. My heart broke a bit. I wanted to be the one she ran to, a chance to be a hero. He was still dressed in his torn workshirt, and she clad in a black teeshirt with some past concert times listed on the back. She had wrapped her arm with a white bandage, yet the blood had soaked through. My father scooped her up and walked to the front door. Her black make-up was smeared down her face.

Mr. Grant grabbed my leg as I passed the living room. I gaped at what was once a man, but now was an arm, shoulder and head. It moaned a nasty sound as I kicked it off me. I could see what the Morslys had been eating until they decided to go out for something fresher. We closed the door behind us.

Pa put her in the seat and I rode in the back, mindful of the tarp, I kept imagining Mike reaching out from the end of the roll and pulling me down into the folds of that blue hell.

As we pulled out of the driveway, I gazed across the field. The town lay in the distance, miles of farmland between. A long column of black smoke, which seemed to come from city hall, stretched to the sky. I stared over the spread of land. I couldn't see the fire but I knew it was there, just as I felt certain that everything had changed forever. Plumes of dust kicked out behind us on the dirt road, filling the space with a hazy vision of the Morsly farm, now truly part of the past.

Looking down, I noticed a puddle of blood forming around my feet. It encircled my right foot and seemed to stop and gel. When my father parked the truck near our front door, I stood up and wiped my boot heel on the tarp. He ran to the passenger side and helped Sarah out. Scooping her back into his arms, he climbed the porch steps. Bumping the door with his hip, it swung open as he entered.

"Jessie, bring the alcohol and bandages from the medicine cabinet. We'll be in my room."

I took the stairs in a bound and fetched the items for him ... for her. I stepped in the bedroom as he unwrapped her arm. The mottled, blackened flesh underneath sent a smell into the air. A slight whiff turned my stomach.

"Damn, it's septic." He sat on the edge of the bed. Sarah held her arm out and had her head turned the other way. He raised his hand to his chin as he looked unseeingly into a corner.

"What does that mean, Pa?"

He didn't answer, but left the room. I heard him rummaging around in one of the kitchen drawers, and then heard him leave the house.

"Sarah?" I touched her shoulder.

"Yeah?" she said very weakly, not turning or looking at me for that matter.

"My dad will get you fixed up good." I hoped my voice was confident enough. Footsteps on the porch made me grab the shotgun, and my father walked in with a board and a propane torch. I relaxed and put the gun back down.

"Take off your belt, Jessie, I'm gonna really need your help." I unbuckled the leather strap from my waist and handed it to him. He took it and fed it under her arm high, then cinched it back onto itself. He pulled it tight and hard. She moaned in pain. The tattoo of a skull, with worms climbing out of an eye socket, distorted with the stretched skin. "Put that board under her arm, right below the elbow." I did what I was told. I just couldn't figure out what he was doing until I saw the cleaver tucked in his waistband.

Producing a match from behind his ear, he struck it with his thumbnail and lit the torch.

"Pa," I whispered, "you gonna cut off her arm?"

He turned the knob on the propane tank until the flame burned a tight blue. "Nope, I'm gonna need to hold her down." His eyes locked onto mine. "You are."

My head spun, my stomach churned, and my eyes welled with tears. My father grabbed my arm and pulled me from the room. I looked back at Sarah. She hadn't moved.

"Boy, you better get your head straight," he scolded. "I don't want to do this either, but if we don't she will die." I felt a huge lump in the back of my throat. I wiped my eyes with the back of my hand and nodded at him.

"What I need you to do is take this cleaver and go pour some alcohol over the blade. Don't get that too close to the torch, you hear?" He slipped the flat blade to me; I looked down into my reflection and saw a wide-eyed and scared boy. As I poured the liquid on the blade in the sink of the kitchen, the image seemed washed away to a confident young man. I hoped that's what I saw. He was still waiting for me outside the room.

"When I hold her down, you swing that thing hard and fast. Try to get it right above the elbow." I nodded my head in agreement. "Jessie, I'm depending on you. Then grab the torch and burn that stump real good or she'll bleed to death, you hear? Real good." Then he walked in before me.

"Sarah? Sarah, sweetheart, we're gonna help you." My father's calm, soothing voice almost made me believe it was going to be easy. She moaned a little, almost like in a sleep. He climbed on the bed, his knees sinking deeply into the mattress. "I'm not gonna lie to you, this is gonna hurt. But it'll be all over soon, then you can be on the mend." Straddling her, he drew a deep breath and nodded at me.

In an instant he grabbed her shoulders and yelled, "Now!" The movement woke Sarah from her haze and she began to buck and scream. I stood frozen, until she sank her teeth into my father's forearm. "Now! Dammit!" he bellowed. And I swung that cleaver as hard and fast as I possibly could. It cleaved clean and without error and buried itself into the board below. She screamed out a cry, releasing my father's arm. Then came the torch. I'd rather cut her arm off twenty times than imagine the pain she was dealing with as I cooked the stump of her arm. It sizzled and smelled like a mixture of burning hair and grilled steak. Then she passed out. I remember thinking how upset Momma would have been to see the mess her sheets were in.

Pa got up, grabbed the alcohol and poured it on his arm. He growled and winced as it burned into his wound. Looking over at the stump of her arm, he treated it too with a raised eyebrow.

"Jessie, you need to wrap that up with clean dressings. I'm gonna go find those pills Doc Ashford gave me when he pulled my tooth. She's gonna be in all sorts of hurt when she wakes up. Maybe those will take the edge off and make it bearable. I hope."

I've noticed when folks are at a loss, they hope and pray. I knew there was a whole bunch of hurting going on that day. The good Lord threw us a curveball, changed the rules in the middle of the game, leaving people unsure of the situation, the future, even their lives. Maybe all that was left was hope. Yet I walk outside my door and the birds still fly, the wind still blows. Here on our piece of land things seemed the same. But death doesn't always come floating in the air or on the wings of the crows. Sometimes death comes in on two feet.

She woke up screaming.

Pa stayed beside her bed all that day, using his voice to calm her. I stood out on the front porch to make sure we didn't get, as my father called them, surprise visitors. Keeping her quieted down with the pain killers, she seemed to sleep so peaceful.

Two days had gone by without incident. I sat on the edge of the porch with the shotgun cradled in my arms. I'd seen folks walking in the distance, but none had come close. My father came outside the door and hunkered down on his haunches next to me. His eyes scanned the horizon for any movement as he sighed.

"She isn't doing so well, burning up with fever. I need to drive into town and see what's left. At least pick up some antibiotics and other supplies." He spoke in a low monotone. "The radio has been playin' nothing but static. I've got to know what's out there before ... well, just let me see."

"I'm alright, Pa. She gonna be out for a while?"

"I 'spect so. She had three of the pills in the last few hours. Probably be sleeping most of today."

I watched the truck as he drove away. I had given him the shotgun to take with him because we had more extra shells for that than the rifle. My father said he'd look for some more ammo while he was in town. The wind was bouncing across the yard again, and the crows cawed in the trees. A rabbit, seeming unafraid, hopped out front of the barn. I raised the sights and thought about the good fried rabbit we could be eating that night. The rifle shook in my grip. I lowered it and watched the animal scurry away.

The door opened behind me.

Sarah came onto the porch, a thin line of snot hanging from her nose. The color was out of her skin, leaving it grey. A haze covered her eyes, but they were just as breathtaking as the first time I had met her. And the most beautiful woman I had ever met wanted me. Her hand rose as she stumbled toward me. Then she fell, and made a couple of unsuccessful attempts to stand. I raised the rifle again. My aim was true. I swallowed hard that lump in the back of my throat.

I mourned her alone, my eyes full of tears. I opened a new tarp and rolled her body in it. She deserved a new tarp. I had made her last days on earth a pure Hell; at least she could have an unused shroud. I said a few words over her body. He watched from behind the wheel of the truck as I lifted her roll into my arms and carried it to my hole. He walked over and grabbed the shovel from me. I watched from the porch as he buried her. He fell to his knees beside her grave. There would be no marker.

The truck's white hood was crumpled and covered with blood. A stack of shotgun shells and rifle ammo occupied the front seat. Several used shells were scattered on the floorboard. The truck was loaded with supplies, mainly canned food and dry goods, nothing that needed to be kept cold. The electric went out the first night. Don't think it'll be back. Luckily we had the propane tank filled the week before, so we could still cook. I looked back at my father; he was kneeling under the tree. If there's one thing I've learned, it's that a man needs to grieve in his own way. I brought the supplies into the house.

He was quiet as we ate dinner, even when I asked about town. We had pulled the truck across the driveway and sunk several posts. Then stretched a roll of chicken wire and fenced us off from the world, from what was left out there. By the look in Dad's eyes, there wasn't much. He didn't speak of that trip.

He would hold his arm and stare into space.

I woke the next morning and brewed a pot of coffee on the stove. Pa never cared for the newfangled electric coffeemakers. We had the oldest percolator in existence, that's what Mom had called it anyway. But it did make good coffee. My father was out in the barn, so I filled a cup for him to drink while I went to fetch some eggs for breakfast. There was somebody at the fence; they weren't trying to get in, just standing there. As I entered the barn I dropped the cup.

Pa was tightening an ankle-cuff to his leg with wrenches, attaching himself to that chain. I cried out in anguish. He looked at me and threw the wrenches toward the workbench, where they clattered on the floor. He stood up off his chair.

"She bit me, boy. We've got to be safe. You've got to be safe."

"But Pa, she bit ya before she turned. You'll be alright. Please! You have to be."

"Just a couple days, and then we'll see ... a week tops. But you have to stay out of my reach. Promise me." He slapped the back of his chair. "Promise me!"

"Okay, but in a week I'm getting you out of here. You just wait ... just wait."

"Sure, Jessie, but how about a cup of that coffee, it smelled good. And how 'bout grabbing one of those roosters for dinner tonight?" He forced a smile. "I sure could use fried chicken today."

"I'll be right back with your coffee. Do you need anything else right now?"

He smirked. "Yeah, I'm gonna need a bucket. Of all things to forget."

"No, Pa, you forgot something else." I went and hugged him tight. He held me so tight, I could feel a tear fall from his face onto my neck.

Mom woulda been proud of us.

I brought a chair and a lantern into the barn that evening for dinner, and we played cards as always. I reached across the table to retrieve the deck. He grabbed my arm and left an imprint of his hand on the side of my face. I fell off my stool, scooting on my backside away, rubbing my cheek. The sting was not as painful as the fact that he hit me for the first time in my life.

"Damn it, Jessie, don't forget your promise. I'm sorry, but you can't get too comfortable. Not after what I saw." He put his hand to cover his eyes. In the light of the lantern, I could see the tears glistening on his cheeks.

"What did you see out there, Pa?" I righted my chair and sat up.

My father sobbed loudly. I slid my handkerchief across the table. He picked it up and dried his eyes. "I've seen things that haunt my dreams. People turning on each other. Cannibalism in the streets. I was managing to deal with it until I saw the Dugans fighting over their baby. I watched in horror as they tore it apart and fought like dogs over the pieces. I lost control and ran over them with the truck. They didn't deserve to exist anymore. There's nothing out there ... the world has changed."

We made two meals off of that rooster. There were still plenty of laying chickens, so we weren't gonna go hungry. Canned beans and something called potted meat product filled our stomachs. Pa had brought cases of these things home. There were always people walking around the outside of the fence. I had seen survival of the fittest in action when they turned on each other. I guess when they got really hungry, it didn't matter what they ate.

Pa was getting a bit grumpy; I believe he was bored. He could reach his horse and spent quite a bit of time grooming her. But one day he was sitting in his chair with his head down on the table. I brought in fresh water and his morning coffee. He had placed his waste bucket out where I could reach it, yet for the first time it had been empty. He had been out here for five days. Only two more.

"Pa?"

My father raised his head, eyes glazed over. He lunged at me. The table blocking him skidded across the floor until it fell on its side. I cried out as reality slapped me hard. I fled the barn. There were four people on the outside of the fence. I sat on the porch with the rifle and shot one in the head. Soon as it collapsed, the others feasted on the corpse. I shot them all. My father wasn't like one of those things ... he wasn't.

I ate dinner by myself that night. I knew my dad would be yelling for his food in the morning. I knew it. I hoped.

There was nobody outside the fence this morning; the bodies must have been dragged off during the night. I brewed a pot of coffee for my father. He was always in a better mood after drinking his morning mud. I walked into the barn with high hopes. The horse backed against the far side of the stall. Animals have a good sense of danger. My father was hungry during the night. He had eaten his left forearm down to the bone. He looked up, chewing, and lunged at me again. The chain grabbed his ankle and yanked him down on his face. He pulled himself toward me as far as the chain would allow. Totally mindless. I ran outside and vomited.

I had stared at the stars many nights from the yard, dreaming. The future isn't here in this land of dirt and seed. There must be others out there like me. I packed the truck with food and ammo, filled it with gas from the hand-pump gas tank. And cut a section of that chicken-wire fence down.

I loaded the rifle and walked back to the barn a couple hours later. The thing in there wasn't my father anymore. My father was the man who held me when I needed him. The man who played cards with me, who talked to me. My father was the person who taught me how to be a man, who showed me the meaning of love.

He was lying on the floor still reaching. The thing that wore my father's face was the great liar. Some invader that took over his body after he was gone. I thought these things. I aimed my rifle; his eyes cleared for a brief moment as he grabbed the barrel and held it to his head. I saw a tear in those dead eyes. I squeezed the trigger.

His agony was over. I could no longer hold back the pain I felt, the anguish a man shouldn't have to deal with. I thought I'd rather die than to suffer that feeling again.

But I'd rather live.

Death Bonds

The twin girls were dead. This was a fact. The bodies were placed in a grotesque fashion with their arms and legs intertwined in an embrace held together with hanger wire. They faced each other, their heads held back by their long, dark brown hair twisted around the wire that secured their feet, mouths opened wide in a scream; a scream that was never heard. Flies swarmed around the gruesome artwork, landing deep inside the gaping maws. The openings gave an echoing effect to the buzzing as the flies continued passing through the wide parted lips. Propped up against the stairway banister with the remnants of bodily fluids gelling beneath them as the carpet soaked up the moisture, the pungent, sickening sweet smell of death filled the vacant house. A sudden breeze through a broken window brought the flies to a swarming cloud before settling back down.

The girls whisper as they wait. Time has no meaning to the dead.

Cliff cursed his luck as the old Buick stalled out again turning onto the driveway leading to the house. Linda rolled her eyes as he turned the key over until the starter took its toll, killing the battery. She stroked the back of his head while Cliff bumped the horn with his forehead. Still with his head on the steering wheel, he turned to look at Linda. Smiling, she crossed her eyes and stuck a finger aside her nose. Laughter soon erupted and filled the Buick with more life than the battery was willing to provide. He leaned over and gave

Linda a quick peck on the lips.

"I'll come back for our things after a while. I'm anxious to see the house." Cliff opened his door and stepped out. A heavy wind blew across his face; he closed his eyes enjoying the moment. "Must be a storm coming," he yelled over the whistling wind in his ears. Shutting her door, Linda examined the oncoming thunderheads.

"By the looks of those clouds, we'd better get moving if we expect to have dry underwear before we get there." Linda scanned the long driveway ahead until it disappeared around a corner. The driveway was an unused path with long golden tufts of grass sprouting up in its tracks. The sides, the same of that beautiful golden-colored grass, slapped noisily upon itself and the dense brush. The wind brought it all to life.

Linda looked at Cliff and smiled: he was still standing at his open door with his eyes closed, letting the wind pass through his hair. He looked so at peace. The air blowing over her sweaty bare arms sent goose bumps down her body. The air-conditioning in the Buick died a couple of hours earlier, leaving them in a foul mood for most of the drive, until they began singing along with the radio. "Caterwauling" Linda had called it as they laughed, and then Cliff had reached over and held her hand.

A fresh start, a new life, a new house ... well, not quite. They needed a fresh start for sure. The pressures of college and working a full-time job had Cliff drinking heavily. He could be a mean drunk if not handled with kid gloves. Instant asshole, just add alcohol. After he had backhanded her and spent a little time in the county jail, he hadn't touched a drink in six months.

Linda's halo was a bit bent too.

She'd had a short and less than satisfying one-time affair with the apartment handyman. Linda had tried to use Cliff's drinking as an excuse, but once she had seen the young man with the tool belt she knew the mistake that was going to happen. She had led him into the bedroom and was quite disappointed as the wrappings were removed from her present. Actually, Linda had never seen one so ... small; then he was on top kissing her sloppily. She swore she never felt a thing and the bastard had even passed gas while he lay on top of her sweating. The whole room stank of his odor. She had changed the sheets and taken a half-hour shower to cleanse him from her body, but her mind was not as easily purified.

A fresh start.

Cliff had toiled over the CPA exam after he received his Bachelor's degree in accounting. When he received his grade, he'd twirled Linda around the room. They kissed and laughed in each other's arms all night.

Cliff's Uncle Ned had sent word to come to his accounting firm. They had a nice little corner office waiting for him. The best thing of all: Uncle Ned had acquired a nice two-story house, perfect for a couple, a little isolated but the price was right. He'd let them live there for free until things got going for them, as long as they did the upkeep; they'd work out the details.

Cliff's mother hadn't talked much about Ned. A black sheep he surmised; every family has one. They had met at Cliff's mother's funeral for the first time about two years ago. Pleasant enough fellow, Linda had thought, but she'd felt uneasy around Ned.

Just two weeks after Uncle Ned's letter, here they were strolling in beautiful Western Oregon, holding hands up the drive. The rain started falling in quarter-sized drops all around them. To Linda it sounded incredibly like a slow, soft beat as it struck the tall grasses that surrounded them. *A wonderful tempo to beginning this new life,* she thought. They broke into a run for the house.

The rain fell in torrents by the time they reached

the house. Excited to see a porch, Linda maps out a fine place for a swing. She could envision sitting and swaying slowly, drinking lemonade from ice-filled glasses. She giggled aloud when she felt the rain running down and tickling the backs of her legs. Cliff looked at her, shaking his head as he continued fumbling with the door lock.

With an audible click, he pushed the door open. A gust of warm air billowed out of the house as if it were exhaling. They both stepped in with rain dripping onto the floor of the foyer from their well-soaked clothes. Under the odor of musty house, Linda could detect the smell of something else.

"Wow, something must have crawled in here and died!" Cliff commented while holding his nose.

"Shit!" Linda exclaimed. "Why'd we mark all the boxes to which room they belonged if the movers were gonna just throw them in a heap inside the door?"

Cliff started opening every window that wasn't being pelted with rain to air the room out while silently wishing he hadn't tipped the movers quite as well as he did. Linda searched until she found the box marked *bathroom* and threw Cliff a towel. Just as he caught it the door slammed behind Linda making her jump. They both looked over at the door and then Cliff smirked at her. Winking at him and grabbing her bathroom box, she headed upstairs.

A beautiful natural stone-faced fireplace was the main focal point of the sitting room. Cliff followed his nose to its wrought-iron andirons and reached up to open the flue. A solid mass fell down inside, brushing his arm with a furry grey pelt. A fine spray peppered Cliff's bare legs when it split open on the edges of the rack below. Holding his breath against the rotting smell, he grabbed both sides of the grate and walked it outside leaving a trail of maggots falling out the mouth of a dead raccoon. The rain had slowed to a pleasant drizzle.

Reaching down, Cliff wiped his soot-blackened hands on the wet grass. As he stood back up he noticed a pair of shadows in the upstairs window. He raced to the house as they pulled away from the window.

"Linda!" he yelled as he ran up the staircase two steps at a time. Searching the rooms, he followed the sound of running water into the bathroom. "Linda? Why didn't you answer me?" Linda let out a slight yell of surprise as she pulled the curtain slightly back from the shower.

"I didn't hear you, what's the matter?"

"Oh, nothing." Cliff fidgeted when he stared at the opaque view of his wife's form through the curtain. "Just shadows I suppose."

"Don't start that shit, you're gonna freak me out!"

Cliff disrobed and entered the shower with her; taking the soap in hand, he smiled. "Let me calm your nerves then."

She took him into her arms and they begun to kiss, too busy to see the pair of shadows in the doorway; too busy to feel the sudden chill in the air, the unseen eyes watching and waiting. The falling water drowned out the sounds of the whispers in the hall.

They spent the rest of the day moving furniture around in the spacious house and after completing their task, the rooms still looked barren. Cliff rubbed the age-worn arm of the sofa while he contemplated the proper placement of the television.

"Wow! Our crowded little apartment disappeared into this place!" marveled Linda.

Gazing around, Cliff nodded in agreement; the house was quite bigger than he'd imagined. "It would be nice to have new furniture, but winter is coming and I believe when the snow starts it will bury our driveway. We're gonna need a four-wheel drive." Linda pouted a little but knew he was right. He smiled at her childish expression. "I called my uncle and he said he'd come by tomorrow to jumpstart the Buick." He rubbed his chin as in deep contemplation. "We might as well drive into town while it's running, park it in a dealer's lot and let it become their problem."

Linda loved when he got this little sparkle of mischief in his eyes.

A sudden rapping at the door had them looking quizzically at each other and Cliff groaned as he stood, his muscles complaining against the workout he'd given them in the last few hours. "I guess accountants aren't built to move furniture," he whined, looking at Linda for sympathy. She was about to respond when the knocking began again and reminded him of the reason he stood up.

As he opened the front door, an old man attempting a grin with red gums and a few brown teeth extended his hand. The dirty cover-alls he wore were accented by a tattered camouflage boonie hat.

"How ya doin', sir?" the haggard old man slurred, "name's Buck." The smell of sweat filled the doorway only to be trumped by a breath that brought tears to Cliff's eyes. Shaking his hand felt like grasping a leather work glove. "I've noticed yer car is blockin' the drive," Buck said with his noxious breath, "but it's gonna get cold soon and I know yer gonna be needin' some firewood." His eyes left Cliff's and looked behind him into the house, seemingly at the foot of the stairway. It wasn't just a glance but a curious stare.

"Yes, I'll be moving the car tomorrow hopefully, and we will be needing a few cords of wood," Cliff bargained. "If the price is right."

Linda scoffed in the room behind him, suddenly imagining Cliff sending a contestant to play Plinko.

"Yep, I 'spect you'll be needin' more than that. By the look of the leaves, it's gonna be a cold un."

"I believe the chimney needs to be cleaned before anything is burned in there," Cliff added.

"Well sir, I can do that fer ya too, fer an extra fifty."

Cliff smiled and shook Buck's hand. "Great!"

Uncle Ned made good on his promise, calling Cliff the next morning and meeting him to start the Buick. Linda gave Cliff a kiss at the door before he walked down to meet his uncle then grabbed her cleaning supplies. With hands on her hips, she blew an errant lock of hair out of her face when she decided where to begin. Linda heard Cliff start the car and listened to the engine drone as he drove away. She breathed a sigh and sat on the arm of the sofa, looking at the challenge of polishing the stairway banister.

Armed with her orange oil, she began bringing the natural wood finish back to life at the foot of the stairs. With her attention on the work, a slight trickle of blood dripped down on the back of her left hand from the rail above. Linda continued rubbing into the deep grooves of the carved wood. Quite proud of her progress, she brushed the hair from her forehead with her blood-covered hand, smearing a crimson streak of wetness across her face. She stared at the back of her hand, mind racing with a sudden fear, and stood up, bringing her eyes level with a child standing on the stair. At first she just saw the top of her dark-brown hair until the girl looked up. Deep eye sockets slowly emptied a yellowing mass, oozing down the child's grey cheeks. The specter lifted its arms and opened its mouth and vomited a swarm of loud buzzing flies onto Linda. Shielding herself, Linda turned to run and was clasped around the waist by a second child. Looking down into the upturned face, she began to scream and was joined by shrilling cries of anguish from all around her. Then there was silence. Swinging open the front door to flee, Linda ran into open arms as she fainted.

Waking, she was confused of her surroundings until remembering everything. Sitting up quickly with her eyes darting around the room, they rested on a dirty set of cover-alls. Buck was stooped in the fireplace with a few different brushes hanging from a homemade belt of rope.

Sensing her stare, Buck looked over at her and grabbed a rag from his pocket and began wiping his hands.

"You gave me quite a scare, ma'am; passed out right in my arms."

Linda's eyes strayed to the foot of the stairs and she began to shiver slightly.

"I laid ya down on yer couch to keep an eye on ya until yer husband came back. I met him down the road a piece and he said you'd be home, fer me to get to work on this chimney." With a devilish grin he added, "I know I'm a good-lookin feller but I've never had a lady swoon at my presence." He let out a small wheezing laugh.

"Did you see the girls?" Linda pleaded, her eyes never leaving the stairway.

Buck's eyes lost their sparkle as his smile faded.

"Girls you say?" His voice deepened and he seemed to lose his 'good-ole-boy' demeanor. "No ma'am, I sure didn't."

Linda looked back over to Buck, sensing the change.

"Sir," she asked, eyeing him suspiciously, "who are they?"

Buck fidgeted and turned his gaze back to the fireplace. "I'm sure I don't know what yer talking about."

"Bullshit! You know something!"

He stared at the floor for a moment before speaking again.

"That was a bit of bad business, ma'am." Buck turned back to her with sadness in his eyes. "Their names were Anna and Alice Harris. A couple of nine-year-old girls who had come up missing probably at least a dozen years or so ago before a big snowstorm that had snowed most folk in around here." Buck looked about and grabbed a small stool and moved it to where he could sit down in front of Linda. "It was odd how their parents had accepted everything with ease, actually didn't seem surprised at all. Of course, they reported the disappearance but that was it. Never called and asked about things, according to the Sheriff." Buck rubbed the back of his neck. "I just can't understand parents like that; I had a son once and I'd do anything to have Eric back."

Linda followed Buck's stare to the foot of the stairs.

He spoke slowly, almost sorrowful. "No one had seen the girls in at least six hours before that storm hit, and the search team stayed out as long as the weather let 'em, but that was long before anyone thought of checking here."

She watched his eyes well up with tears.

"Come springtime thaw I came up to check on the house for the owner and found them." A tear escaped Buck's eye and he wiped it away. "I swear I heard them calling me."

"So you're telling me that two girls died in this house?" Linda could feel her stomach knotting.

"No ma'am, they were murdered." He closed his eyes tightly and wiped his nose along the sleeve of his cover-alls before he continued.

"Found 'em right over there," he motioned with his head toward the stairs, "all trussed up with wire and in a pretty bad state." He exhaled loudly, emitting a pungent breath that made Linda cough slightly.

"I 'spect the cold kept 'em pretty well with no heat in the house. When the warmer times came," Buck looked up at Linda, "well, we'll leave it at that."

Linda heard a vehicle pull up the driveway, and Buck jumped back to the fireplace to make himself busy when Cliff walked in.

"Baby, come see!" Excited as a schoolboy, with his eyes gleaming, he looked at Linda. Confused by the distress on her face, his eyes narrowed and she could see the ire building up as he headed straight towards Buck.

"What did this son of a bitch do to you?" he bellowed, grabbing Buck out of the fireplace by his cover-alls. "What did you do to her?" he yelled into the man's face. Buck went limp in terror as Linda jumped up and grabbed her husband by the shoulder.

"He hasn't done anything, let him go!" Linda pleaded with tears flowing from her eyes.

Turning and staring in her face, he let Buck loose and grabbed Linda into his arms, holding her tightly.

"Tell me, baby, tell me what's wrong." Cliff's voice wavered. "Please tell me."

Buck regained his composure and slowly walked to the door.

"Excuse me, folks, I'll be outside cleaning the stack," Buck said meekly, and he closed the door behind himself.

Cliff raised her chin in his hand and looked into Linda's eyes. "Now baby, what happened?"

Buck stood a ladder against the eave of the house to give him adequate room to sweep the chimney. Still shaking, he ascended, keeping his balance when the ladder bounced off the edge of the house and returned back safely with each step. Grabbing the rope tied to his belt, Buck quickly raised the pole with the splayed brush on the end. He stared at the horizon and sighed before he turned back to the chimney, turning to the faces of pretty dark-haired girls.

"She's the one, we want her." Alice Harris smiled.

Buck closed his eyes and shook his head. "Please!"

Opening his eyes, he was alone again with the strong smell of rotting flesh filling his nose. Waiting until the breeze took the foul odor away before returning to his work, Buck wished for his anguish to end. He wished his son had never played with those evil little girls, that he'd been stronger; wished his son had never found the gun from the nightstand ... little bitches had talked Eric into killing himself.

Buck was sorry he had gotten so drunk and talked to his old friend. The sadistic bastard had been all too willing to help. He hadn't known it would go as far as it did. Hadn't known the man would leave the girls there to die, or how the twins' mother had smiled at Buck every time he'd seen her afterwards. *Just wasn't proper*, Buck thought, *not proper at all.* He wept for the young couple below as he cut the telephone line coming to the house, but a man needs his son and they'd promised him Eric once they got what they wanted. Above his head the storm clouds rumbled in approval. Buck looked up at the sky before descending the ladder. It was promising to be quite a night. He reached into the pocket of the cover-alls and brought out a cell phone. Flipping it open, he dialed.

"Hello, Ned? It's Buck ... "

Cliff listened as Linda recalled the events of the day to him. His eyes were drawn to her lips as she spoke; only once did he look away to the foot of the stairs.

"I can't stay here!"

Suddenly irritated, Cliff stood up and looked down at her. "Where are we supposed to go? I mean, we have to move now because you inhaled too many cleaning vapors and listened to the rantings of some old man?" He loomed above her with his hands held up in a gesture of extreme exclamation.

"Didn't you hear what I said? I was attacked!" Linda's eyes were wide, disbelieving what he was saying. "I wasn't high on chemicals, it really happened!"

"Would you listen to yourself?" Cliff had a

discrediting look in his eyes that she knew all too well. "If something like that had happened here, don't you think Uncle Ned would've told us?"

Linda glared at Cliff and then at the back of her hands. "I'm feeling sick; I'd like to lie down."

Cliff stroked her cheek with the back of his hand and wiped a tear as it fell. "That's a good idea, why don't you lay down and I'll go have a chat with Buck."

In sudden realization, Linda's eyes flew open in panic. "No! Please don't leave me alone!"

"Calm down, I'll be right outside the door. I'll come running at the slightest sound, I promise."

She stared at the foot of the stairs as she lay down on the couch. Without a word she turned her back to him, shutting Cliff out; shutting out the world.

Cliff looked down at her and sighed lightly then walked to the door.

"Cliff?" Linda said without looking over to him. He stopped and glanced back.

"Yes?" Cliff tried to keep calmness in his voice.

"You do believe me, right?" After a short pause she began to sob as she heard the door close.

The Grand Cherokee stood in the driveway near the door where Cliff had been so excited to present it to his wife. He could recall seeing it on the lot and how the gloss-black finish had won his heart immediately. It was parked with its hood open, and a cover-all covered backside bent over the engine compartment.

"WHAT THE HELL ARE YOU DOING?" Cliff exclaimed as he grabbed the shoulder of the man and spun him around. In Buck's grasp were a handful of wires. Cliff's face turned red as he looked at the long black wiring and back up to Buck's face.

"I'm sorry, sir." Buck's gaze slowly rose.

Cliff's eyes widened in surprise when he looked down to see the handle of a large screwdriver protruding from his own chest.

"I truly am sorry, sir." There were indeed tears running down the man's face.

Cliff turned back to the house; two girls sat cross-legged on the porch giggling at him. He coughed and a spray of blood covered his lips, dripping in long tendrils onto the front of his shirt. A large bloom of blood spread across his favorite polo shirt; the one Linda had bought for his last birthday. The girls stood together and held hands, then walked through the still-closed front door.

Cliff attempted to yell out but was unable to. He stumbled to the porch as the door opened and fell across the threshold at Linda's feet.

She screamed, and then looked up at Buck.

"I just wanted them to understand the pain they caused; he said he'd show them." Buck looked at Linda with hope of her understanding. "He said he'd show them."

"GET AWAY FROM US, YOU BASTARD! " Linda screamed and dragged her husband into the house. She glanced up at Buck, expecting him to be climbing the steps, but he just stood and watched.

"I'm sorry. He said he'd show them."

Heart pounding fast, she rushed to the phone in the kitchen.

Cliff opened his eyes, unable to speak, unable to ask for forgiveness. They were standing over him. "Hurts, don't it?" a beautiful little dark-haired girl asked and giggled.

Cliff coughed as his lungs filled with blood.

"It's nothing compared to the pain of slowly rotting." The girls laughed loudly as their skins started to slide off. It looked like removing a glove to him, slapping the floor as it fell, leaving large loose piles of skin around their legs. Cliff tried to scream, spewing up red foam just as they faded away.

The echoes of their laughter trailed off in his ears as he died.

Linda returned from the kitchen armed with a large carving knife.

"NO!" She screamed, dropping to her knees next to Cliff's head. Cradling it in her lap and weeping loudly; searching his face and hoping for any sign of life.

A knocking caught her breath. Shaking wildly, she stared at the door.

He weeps for the sacrifice of her body and her mind. When Buck had gone back in the house later on that day, he wasn't sure she was even alive. She was still wired to the stairs with those damn coat hangers, but totally mindless. She is not bound to the bed, and in Buck's opinion, she is quite healthy. "Linda?"

She laid Cliff's head down gently and slowly backed away from the door. The knife in her hand clanked on the floor as she crawled away.

"Linda? It's Ned."

In a wave of relief, Linda began to sob loudly as she hopped up. She ran to the door and with her hand on the lock she stopped.

"Ned, are you alone?"

"Yes, what's going on? Where's Cliff?"

Linda opened the door and ran crying into Ned's arms when he entered.

"That horrid man killed Cliff. There was nothing I could do."

Ned looked down at Cliff's blood spreading into the carpeting.

"Calm down, I'll take care of this."

He took the knife from her shaking hand and helped her sit down on the bottom step of the stairs before walking to the closet. Reaching in, he pulled out a couple of coat hangers and started to unwind them.

"Buck!" Ned called out, "get rid of that." He motioned at the dead body as the old man entered the front door.

"OH NO!" Linda cried as she turned to crawl up

the stairs. She made it three steps until she ran into the bare feet of two children. She looked up to see them grinning before they faded away.

"Come here, little lady!" He pulled her back by a handful of her hair. "It's your lucky day!"

"LET GO OF ME, YOU SICK SON OF A BITCH!" Linda screamed out, opening her eyes long enough to see Buck dragging her husband's body out the front door. He looked into her eyes and sighed deeply then closed the door.

Linda gazed into Ned's face as he spoke, her mouth quivering in terror.

"All we wanted to do was scare them, but they just laughed at us. Things got out of hand and they died; giggled and whispered to each other the whole time." Ned gripped her arm and bent a wire around her wrist, twisting it tightly. "Then the giggling stopped and they started speaking in some language I've never heard before and then a deeper laughter began, a noise that had no business coming from a couple of little girls. Spooked me so I just left. I'd planned on coming back and cleaning up later, but the weather didn't cooperate."

"Please!" Linda pled.

Ignoring her, he continued, "That night and ever since then, they have been tormenting me." Ned bent close to her face. "Imagine, sleepless nights for twelve years, with no sign of it ending ... bedroom always smelling like road kill." He paused thoughtfully a moment. "Visions of Hell they showed me in my dreams." Linda could smell the scotch on his breath. "I was on the verge of insanity until they whispered in my ear." He stood back from her, spread his arms and smiled. "All we have to do is give them what they want," Ned gave her a quick wink, "and what they want is you."

"Why me?" Linda sobbed as she laid her chin on her chest. "WHY ME?" she screamed, jumping up only to be held back down.

"Calm down, pretty lady, that's no way to act for a woman in your condition."

Linda's face grew ashen. "What do you mean?"

Ned didn't answer but continued twisting the wire to the banister. "Now, just relax, I'm sure it will make it easier."

"Make what easier?"

Ned laughed, "I don't know, but I don't want to watch!"

He looked down and seemed content with the bindings. "You two were perfect for their plans." He said as he squats down, "No family except a distraught Uncle Ned, who will swear you never arrived." He looked up the stairs over Linda's head. "Now, my sweet, I'll leave you to get acquainted. They are gonna love you." Ned stood, only looking back once, then walked out the door.

Linda could sense someone behind her and turned her head. Breathing in deep hitches, she saw only shadows on the wall, until her hair was pulled straight back. The pungent sweet smell of rot attacked her senses as the twins appeared in front of her. They looked at each other and, in unison, bent over Linda, covering her face with their long black hair. She could feel her mouth filling with a vile stinging fluid. She coughed up to expel it, as a rotting hand covered her mouth.

"Swallow, bitch!" a voice from the pits of Hell ordered.

Linda had no choice but to obey.

The picturesque trees, with their red and orange leaves falling, were soon bare. As time passed, a blanket of white covered the landscape. The house, devoid of color, rested silently.

Ned slept through the night again, and in the beginning of May he didn't wake back up. The doctor ruled it a massive coronary. He was quite a wealthy man with no family, except a nephew.

In the heat of summer, Buck stands over a bed. He looks down at the prone figure and cleans the wastes from the plastic sheets. A once-beautiful woman moans lightly on the bed, the only sound she has made in many months. She stares unblinking at the ceiling. A feeding tube is in her throat; she gagged on it for a few days, but got used to it quickly. Buck sits every day talking to her. He thinks maybe she understands him sometimes, maybe she listens.

He pulls down the sheet as her legs start kicking, revealing her nakedness and protruding belly. She makes a grunt and opens her mouth to scream, but there is no sound. Buck watches with awe at the forms within wrestling for position. Linda's back arches and she finally screams as claws appear, running down the length of her belly from inside. Blood sprays the plastic sheets as miniature hands tear their way out of the birth canal. A loud crack reports and Linda wails once again as the infant pulls its head out amid a pool of blood. Squirming its shoulders past next, using the blood as a lubricant, it emerges. Its umbilical cord pulls tight, Buck realizes a second baby is using it to pull itself into the world. As its head appears, it twists and kicks out. He picks up and cleans the newborns and places them on Linda's milk-swollen breasts, then cuts the umbilical cords with his pocket knife. The babies drink greedily. Buck knows Linda won't last through the day and looks over at the five cases of formula; he hopes it is enough. He smiles. The girls are beautiful. Buck backs up in amazement as Linda's belly stretches further than he thinks possible.

The infants open their eyes and giggle as a third whispers from between her legs.

Linda screams again as her legs split open wide, falling off the sides of the bed, only connected by skin.

A large figure pulls itself from out of the gore, sliding down the plastic and stepping away from the end of the bed. Its foot wrapped in Linda's entrails dragging behind like a gruesome streamer, it advances toward Buck. The girls giggle even louder when their new mother's insides slide down and splatter on the hardwood floor. Buck smiles wide as he looks into the face of his son, but the boy gives no sign of recognition. Buck sits on the floor and pulls Eric onto his lap, whispering his love to the boy, holding and kissing the top of his head. Then grimaces in pain and embracing his son tightly as Eric sinks his teeth into Buck's left thumb. Buck rocks him in his arms as Eric chews noisily. *Sacrifices must be made,* Buck thinks as he holds his bloody hand to Eric's face.

A growing boy needs to eat.

I.C.U.

The woman woke, sight blurred by the hair hanging over her eyes. A shadow came closer and with one finger moved it to the side. He wanted her to see, waiting until she woke. She whimpered through the rag tied tightly on her face. Brown eyes, welled with tears and filled with fear, stared into his own. Chuckling lightly, he walked to the window and drew the blind, not wanting to have any prying eyes. If her mouth hadn't been gagged, she would have screamed when he came closer.

She had tried.

Simon sat out in his car in front of his mother's house and finished his beer. Belching, he opened the door. Hinges screeched in protest as he scrunched the can and threw it into the gutter. It was nice to come home after work and just shut out the world, if only for a few hours.

A little solitude.

"I told you to stay out of my room, Ma." Simon towered over the frail woman.

Janice Hardwick's black hair, now splashed by the grays of time, was pulled neatly into a bun. Her deep blue eyes washed out by the decades stood staring up almost defiantly. "I was just bringing in your clothes."

"I don't care, you wait till I get home." Simon did not like this defiance. His father had taught him how to take care of these things and his mother knew it.

"I'm sorry, pork chops tonight?" She tried to change the subject with his favorite meal; meatloaf was on her mind, but that was before. She would walk into town for some chops so he wouldn't be angry.

"Yeah, sure." He let it go this time and sneered as her face flushed in relief. *This time,* Simon thought while raising the back of his hand to the side of his face. He rubbed it across the scruff from a three-day-old growth of stubble. The movement made her flinch. "Applesauce too, I want applesauce."

She nodded then hurried down the hall as he closed the door, chuckling to himself. *Pork chops, third time this week. Dad would have been proud.*

Simon stripped off his light-green scrub top. He was a medical orderly at Borse County Hospital (he preferred the title Ward Assistant). Being a large, strong man, he had no trouble moving patients and "handling" problems. Actually, he enjoyed that part. A good pinch on the back of the neck was enough to defuse most situations. Dad had shown him that move too. He was his father's son. Dad knew how to handle things quite well. He didn't take guff from anyone. An accident on the loading docks where he had worked had taken him from Simon. He had slipped (pushed?) between the moorings, and as he tried to climb out the ship crushed him against the pier. It seemed too convenient, too many witnesses all pointing the blame at his father. Simon had an issue with this, knowing his dad had been around those docks all his life. He knew better. Fault or not, it had happened on the job so his mother received a hefty Workman's Comp check. She was able to pay off the mortgage and have a nice nest egg stashed away in the bank. Free room and board; Simon had no difficulty filling his father's shoes at home. To keep Mom in line ... to handle things.

He heard the front door close and watched his mother from the window facing the street as she started her way to the market a half mile down the block. He hoped she got the right applesauce and not the store-brand crap or she'd be making a trip back to the market real soon. He looked up at the sky. *Have to keep an eye on that.* If it started raining, he would drive to the store to pick her up. Couldn't have his food getting ruined, but she needed to learn to bring an umbrella. After just working a twelve-hour shift, he sat on the bed and promptly went to sleep. As the rain fell.

"Simon?" Tapping on the door. "Simon, are you awake? Dinner is ready."

"Yeah, yeah, YEAH, FOR CHRIST SAKE, I'M AWAKE! COULD YA QUIT BEATING ON THE DAMN DOOR?!!"

"It's just that dinner is ready and I know you don't like your food getting cold."

"Well then, ya need to keep it warm, don't you? I'll be down in a minute."

She was sitting to eat when he walked in. Scanning the table, his eyes fixed on the jar in the middle.

"Generic applesauce? Really, Mom?"

She sighed.

"This time bring your umbrella," Simon added.

By the time she returned, he had finished eating. He'd even tried some of the applesauce and found it wasn't that bad, so he ate half the jar. She had only cooked three chops though, barely enough for him. He went up the stairs as she began to clean the table. Later the microwave chimed when her TV Dinner was ready. Meatloaf with corn and mashed potatoes. She had gotten used to eating alone.

The next day, Simon felt the bile rise in his throat as he was pre-op shaving the excessively hairy groin of an old man. Although he wore gloves, this part of the job thoroughly disgusted him. But it was necessary for cardiac catheterization, and he had to do it a couple times a week. Simon had come to the conclusion that the elderly didn't bathe regularly. There were all sorts of odors that rose from their nether regions. What made it worse was the man hummed to himself while Simon dealt with his unkempt groin. Holding his breath, he completed the job. And the humming continued.

In the restroom afterwards, Simon cupped his hands under the running water and splashed it over his face. Cool liquid dripped down his nose back into the basin. The stench of the unwashed man slowly faded from his nose but not his memory. Pursing his lips and blowing, a spray of water blew a mist into the air. Small drips of water spread large spots onto his scrubs.

Simon was suddenly aware of a man standing behind him, also wearing scrubs, the same light-green uniform that was the color for all positions except doctors and nurses. Another orderly, he surmised. Odd, he had never seen this guy before. Simon reached for a towel to wipe his face and the man was gone. There was a stirring in one of the stalls. He headed out of the bathroom. Simon had endured enough smells without adding more.

It was about time for his shift to end. Simon left the hospital as the secondhand swept the twelve. Digging into his pockets he found the keys to his car. As he walked, he saw the face of the man in the bathroom through a windshield. The guy just leered back.

Jake had left early to watch the ladies leave. This orderly job was the best he'd ever had. Pretty much did as he pleased. Long as his work got done, they left him alone. It bothered Jake that the man in the bathroom stared at him for so long, and now the bastard was gawking again.

When he was bent over the sink with water dripping from his nose, the jerk-off looked like a fool. It would have been so simple just to grab the back of his head and introduce his face to the sink spout. It always amazed Jake how easily the face caved in under pressure. He'd have to keep a watch on him. Maybe the prick needed a lesson to keep his eyes to himself. Jake smiled. The idea sent a wave of pleasure through his arms and legs. Happy thoughts always did, and the really good ones made him erect. He turned the keys in the ignition and rubbed his hand across his groin before driving out of the parking lot. He watched the nurses in his rearview mirror. He found them extremely sexy, especially the middle-aged ones. Once they got too old, he couldn't stand to look at their haggard faces. But these were off-limits, couldn't risk it, not here. *Don't shit where ya sleep.* Jake gripped his erection through his pants and smirked. *So who's gonna be the lucky lady tonight?*

A little Diazepam injection had Cindy Gentry staring at Jake until her knees buckled. He had watched her loading clothes into a dryer and shoving change into the machine. She nodded at Jake as he came in, probably relieved not to be alone in this neighborhood. The 24-hour laundromat wasn't in the best of areas. Jake walked to the soda machine and bought a bottled water, twisting the cap and taking a big swig as he stepped back outside. She came through the door a few minutes later, thumping the top of a new pack of cigarettes. The needle entered at the base of her neck. The cigarettes fell. Jake's eyes followed the unopened package to the ground. Cindy did nothing, her mind not putting together what had just happened. Jake reached down and picked up the smokes. Lucky day, his brand. She fell limp into his arms. With the dose he gave her, she would be out for hours. Jake laid her gently into the trunk of his car. With that, Mrs. Cindy Gentry became a statistic. The 39-year-old mother of four went missing forever when the trunk closed.

Simon woke on his bed. Mom had made some cheap excuse for meat and spent most of the afternoon picking the stuff off the floor and walls. She knew better than to piss him off with some shit that resembled dog food. She knew better. It was her own damn fault she had to clean it out of the rug. Dad wouldn't have put up with stained carpets. Not in his home. Simon would check in the morning before work. He looked across the room at the window and could see the man in the next building. *Son of a bitch,* he thought, *it's that guy from the hospital.* He was kissing a lady. Simon couldn't see much of her; she was lying on a bed. Through squinted eyes he watched as the man disrobed and straddled the woman. Simon watched for a while, as the man roughly took her, before he drifted back to sleep.

Jake had made a real mess with this one. He had waited until she woke up to use her for his needs. She was exactly the type he liked. Even though she wept and cried out into her gag, she reached orgasm quickly. She had fought it but succumbed to his fingers. Jake was almost sad to destroy her ... almost. Using a scalpel, he crosshatched the skin on her chest. The blade was so sharp, she hardly uttered a sound as he made the incisions. With a pair of needle-nose pliers he gripped the corners of the skin and peeled up perfect little squares. She wasn't so silent then. The straight cuts, leaving ragged holes of meat underneath, bled profusely.

Jake pumped his penis hard between her tied spread-eagled legs as she screamed into the rag in her mouth. Her pain was exquisite. Her inner muscles cinched down on his member at every scream. He was on the fourth square and nearing his own climax when she defecated. The smell reached his nose and enraged him. He promptly buried the tips of the pliers into her left eye and pushed. She quit moving soon after that. Jake hopped up to wash the feces from his testicles. Nasty fucking bitch had no right to soil his bed. Though it had plastic covering, it was the principle. He masturbated on her face, filling the eyesocket with his semen. No sense having blue balls too. Damn shame, he was gonna go for Round Two with her.

Across town, the gurney wheel wavered to and fro in a gleaming hospital corridor as the orderly pushed William Jennings. The man had passed away in the night from complications during a heart bypass. Marge the nursing supervisor tossed Jake the morgue key as he snapped his fingers. The underside of the cart held the bagged remains of Cindy Gentry; actually, three 25-gallon biohazardous waste bags. He had found a box of them in a supply closet and kept them in his trunk. On a couple trips to his car with the large duffle bag he carried daily, it was a breeze bringing her into the hospital. As he made his way down to the morgue, he deposited the red sacks with an odd-shaped star inside the disposal bins bearing the same symbol. They were to be picked up later and taken to a crematorium and never seen again. No DNA, no body, no problem. It had become so easy over time. No one even batted an eye. Jake found a quiet little spot in the laundry area to lie down. The long night had caught up with him, and he figured he'd take a nap. Nobody would see and if they did, so what? He had caught most of them down here fucking somebody at one time. A nice quiet place

Belching inaudibly, Simon upturned the soda he had found in the Employees Lounge. The refrigerator was a buffet if it was handled correctly. Could never take too much at once, the natives got restless. Occasionally if there were people on break when he came in, he would have to purchase something from the snack machine or go to the hospital cafeteria and buy a meal. But the cola had been half empty and wouldn't be missed. With the half sub that had been in there since last night, Simon had a good meal without costing a cent again. A nurse came in as he was wadding up the sandwich wrapper. She was a pretty thing, and he enjoyed watching her bend over into the fridge.

"Damn, it's gone." She was shaking her head slightly closing the door. The movement caused a strand of dark hair to fall across her face. "I hate that. People can't buy their own stuff." She turned to Simon. He diverted his eyes quickly as it had been realized he was staring at her backside. Crunching the wrapper tightly in his hand to make sure she didn't see it, he nodded.

"Yeah, I have problems all the time with that. My lunch is gone most of the time too." Looking her in the face, he lost his breath. Eyes that stared right through him; he felt his knees grow weak. Simon couldn't think. He cast his gaze down onto her nametag. Eliza Monroe smirked at his uneasiness.

"Well, umm ..." – she reached and lifted his nametag – "... Simon J. Hardwick, it is nice to meet you." She gave his chest a playful pat. "I'm gonna go down to the cafeteria to get lunch. See ya around, I hope."

Simon managed a nod and, realizing he was breathing from his mouth, grinned like a fool. He watched as she turned for the door. She had been playing with him, actually flirting. Two young nurses walked in before she left, deep within their own conversation. Eliza stood out of the way while they passed and gave Simon a smile as she left. He went to the door and watched her walk down the hall until a man pushing a gurney blocked his view. He looked back at the two nurses talking and left the lounge. Her eyes burned into his memory.

Janice was quite surprised when Simon got home. She hadn't ever heard him whistling when he came in before. She always hid in her sewing room or the kitchen. It was easier that way; he generally was in a better mood after he cleaned up before dinner. Staying busy with cooking or such was always safer. He was a headstrong boy, but he didn't hit her quite as often as his father. She had raised him the best she could. He sure was his father's son though. The wall was lined with pictures of the two together playing football, fishing, and that awful year he learned to box. They would come home nights coughing and wheezing and laughing how the other was such a (sigh) pussy. At the end of the hall was a framed valentine Simon had made for her. He was seven at the time. She cherished it. Red construction paper hearts of three shades poorly cut out and glued on top of each other. In a scrawl was two letters: MA. It was the last beautiful thing she had.

She once was a gorgeous woman; all the boys called on her. Janice's father was quite strict and sent them away with their tails between their legs. Lawrence Hardwick was chatting with her dad when she came home from school one day. According to Father, he was a bright lad with a strong future on the shipyards. Being her last year of high school, it was time for her to do what all proper ladies do. Janice found the young man brash and very arrogant. When they went on a date, he groped at her between shots of whiskey from a flask. He stole her money and her virginity in the same night. Yet, Father welcomed him, and gave his consent the second week.

The first time he beat her was the wedding night. Lawrence was drunk and being obnoxious as he brought her to his apartment. The roaches scurried into dark hiding spots between the walls. The place stank of urine and rotten food. The ceiling was watermarked from leaks, and the toilet was disgusting. He caught her curling her lip, and he had fattened it. As she lay crying, he raped her before passing out. She snuck away and ran home, but Dad told her to go home to her husband. Janice was his problem now.

She privately rejoiced when her father died.

He smiled at the table and didn't inquire about what brand of sauce or expiration dates. Simon ate quickly but, for the first time she could remember, inquired about her day and cleared the table when they finished. Feeling a lump in the back of her throat, she sat and stared at him. A flood of tears came rolling down her cheeks. Simon grinned before stopping and handing her a napkin. He hugged her. Janice sobbed in his arms. Careful not to wet his shirt with tears, she wiped her face and smiled at him. To her this was Simon, not the beast her husband had created. This was the boy that made the valentine. Lawrence hadn't changed everything.

Simon squatted down in front of her. "Ma, I met someone. I can't describe how she makes me feel. I'm gonna ask her out tomorrow." He held her face between his hands. "I love you, Ma." Kissing her gingerly on the forehead. She embraced her son, hoping he had come home for good. They cleaned the dishes together and talked. He spoke of this new lady with a spark in his eyes that had never been seen in this household. Laughing and smiling, he told how nervous he had been. Janice pulled him to her and embraced him again tightly.

The Hardwick house curtains were opened for the first time since they were put up. Lawrence liked the gloominess of a darkened room. Janice hadn't dared to open them before. But today was different, she had her son back. The sun cut into the parlor, leaving wide rays of light cast upon the walls. She sat on the sofa and smiled. Maybe she would talk to Simon about new furniture. There was plenty of money in the bank account, and it would be so nice to have something new and start afresh. She turned on the radio and danced. Her body floated gracefully through the room. It was a beautiful day. She felt ... young again.

Blowing across his arm, Jake watched the hair dance in his breath. Bored. He tried to watch television, but the same crap was always on. Soap operas, daytime talk and infomercials just made him turn it back off. He thought of going to find another bit of fun but it was too soon, couldn't press his luck quite that much. Besides, the hours of dismembering the body and getting rid of it weren't worth the hour of pleasure he received ... yet. He inhaled deeply and blew. He had tried power tools, but they were noisy and made more of a mess. No, for cutting them up, nothing beat a hacksaw in the bathtub. He knew just how to divvy up the body parts so they'd fit in the bags. Arms, feet and head in one, legs into another. If they had been really good, he'd have sex with the abdomen before it got cold, just for the memory. Jake blew ...

Keeping a breath mint on hand all morning, Simon also kept his eye out for the lady that had stolen his heart in a single glance. His demeanor was being noticed by all. Some that had given him a wide berth before now were starting conversations. Exchanging pleasantries was never one of his strong suits. But the "Good morning" and the "Have a nice day" flowed out of his mouth so easily. He even joined in a "High Five" but really didn't care for that. He realized the nurses weren't pawning off all the shit-jobs on him. A smile goes a long way.

Eliza came into the Employees Lounge shortly after eleven. Simon was quick to make his presence known and invited her to a hot meal in the cafeteria on him. She surveyed the contents of a brown paper sack from the fridge then nodded agreement. Tossing the lunch sack into a garbage can, she led the way. Simon was in heaven. He listened to her ramble on about the other nurses in her ward. His eyes never left her face, only hearing half of what she was saying. Didn't matter, her eyes told him so. He couldn't contain his glee when she accepted to have dinner with him this weekend. She giggled to see him smiling so big.

Janice had a large dinner set out when Simon came home. The look on his face gave away his good news. He laughed heartily and they talked all through dinner. Janice hinted at new furnishings but didn't want to seem too pushy. After dinner they watched a movie together on television. Something silly that didn't make much sense. But they enjoyed a bowl of popcorn and they laughed together. Yeah ... together.

He had been sleeping too much. Really needed to get back to work. Didn't go today, he just wasn't feeling right. But he decided to take another nap. Tonight was gonna be a long one. He had needs and they were building. He was gonna have to go out, taste what the city had to offer. The bars were always filled with lost souls looking for love. Funny how they thought they could find it in alcohol, or perhaps it deadened the senses, hiding their pain. Jake fed off it and found it quite delicious at times. So damn appetizing.

And his hunger burned.

She was older, hell, a lot older than she looked in the dim bar. Jake had sat on a stool as the low-class dregs mingled around him. Never spoke a word, just drank a couple beers and watched. Jake was great at watching ... She was across the room; just left a pool table and finished her beer in a long swig. When he observed her leave the tavern, he picked up his keys and departed too. After walking out the door, he saw her duck behind a car. Jake strolled in the general direction until a young couple entered the bar, deserting the parking lot. He snuck up to her as she was urinating behind an automobile. The Diazepam worked quickly with the alcohol in her system. Soon she was in the car. He could see the age on her face but damn, he needed this.

Didn't even wait until she woke. Jake threw her on the bed and cut her clothes from her body. Time and gravity hadn't been kind to this one. Her breasts fell down between her arms. Reminded Jake of tube socks full of sand. Raping her hard and fast, he put a pillow over her wrinkled face so he wasn't reminded of the age. Pounding into her, she awoke. With one hand on the pillow, her screams muffled, he drove a hunting knife repeatedly into her chest as he reached orgasm. He threw the pillow aside and spat down on her face. It hadn't been worth it. Not a good memory, and he just wanted her gone. As he gazed across the room, he saw the eyes in the window watching from the next building.

And he recognized the face.

A glimpse, that's all it took. Simon had watched in horror as the man repeatedly buried the knife into the lady. It was a lady, wasn't it? His head swam. He just happened to wake up to use the restroom when he saw it through the window. Then the man saw him, yeah, their eyes met. Just like before in the bathroom at work. Time stopped for a moment. Simon's bladder had to be dealt with first. Didn't involve him, so let that weird son of a bitch do what he wanted. Gonna keep an eye on him though. When he returned, there was nothing to see. His mind told him, it couldn't possibly have been a woman. It was the sleep in his eyes, that's all. He lay back down in bed. Couldn't possibly have been, he thought as unconsciousness fogged his memory. His smile returned as he dreamt of Eliza's smile.

He watched from the darkened room. Jake's heart raced, wondering how he could have been so stupid. Was the urge so bad, he didn't feel the need to be cautious? He spied the man go back to bed and chortled to himself. Waiting for half an hour, until he was sure nothing was happening. No police beating on the door ... this time. Maybe the guy hadn't seen anything. Lip curling, scowling at the woman lying on the bed with her legs splayed open and the knife protruding from her chest. There would be no time to get rid of this one normally; really wasn't worth the effort. He would take her to the harbor and drop her body between a moored tanker and the docks. Hopefully the current and the rocks below would rid him of this carcass. There were many things in the ocean that would love to have a fresh meal. Jake sneered and whispered, "Wasn't even a decent fuck. The crabs will feast well tonight, anyway."

Eliza's eyes were crying. She was begging for help, yet he just watched as the man cut her throat. The blood bubbled around the blade of the knife, and then sprayed in a last attempt to scream. Her hand outstretched ... Simon woke from the nightmare. Breathless, he sat up on the edge of the bed. Sleep had been a chore last night. Godawful dreams haunted him.

Peering at the window as he walked to the bathroom, there was no movement. No sign of life. He turned on the water in the tub before staring into the mirrored medicine chest. Mornings weren't his best times. A steaming hot shower ought to help, he hoped. In the drone of the water he could still hear her screams. As it splashed upon his head, he leaned on the white tile wall. It tickled as it ran off his nose.

The water continued to fall outside. Gray clouds hung low in the sky.

"Hey, close those Goddamn drapes. What are we running, a peep show?" Giving his mother a glance that she interpreted as "It had better be a pork chop night", he left. She wept as the door closed.

Simon drove quickly to the hospital. He yearned to know it was just a dream, needed to see her.

The air sang electric with the lightning etched across the horizon, crackling the radio with each strike. Thunder vibrated the car as he pulled into the parking lot. The light-green scrub's shoulders were darkened with the pummeling rain before he made it into the hospital's entrance.

His frantic eyes were not welcomed with salutations at the desk. Rushing down the hall, stomach feeling like gelatin, he stopped with his shoulder against the wall. Eliza was leaving a room with a clipboard in her hand. She gave him a confused look as she walked by. His heart slowed. It had all seemed so real. He turned back to the nurses' desk with a grin for her on his face, and they all smiled back. Idiots.

Jake was glad to be at work for a change. He had too much time off lately, and nothing wrong with enjoying your job. Making himself busy cleaning out the sharps containers in rooms; couldn't let those fill up too much or the junkies would be scrounging around in them looking for usable hypodermic needles. Doctors and nurses didn't seem to care. They only sought the cure. Jake had seen the disease, he knew how to cure it. He dumped a bucket into a bin on the cart and went to the next room.

"Orderly!" Jake looked up to see a quite pretty nurse beckoning him.

"Yeah?" He was ready to do something else anyway, and she looked like the type he'd do it with.

"Can you help me get Mr., umm," she consulted her clipboard, "Mr. Johns onto a gurney, please? He's due in X-ray."

"Yes ma'am, sure thing." Jake smiled nice and polite. This nurse was a real looker. He felt his loins stirring deeply. The smell of coconut was light around her. He was sure her skin was as soft and smooth as it appeared. He helped her slide the rotund patient onto the cart.

"Will that be all? I mean, do you need help getting him to the lab?"

"No, that's alright, but thanks." Her smile was delicious. Jake would have to make an exception for this one. It didn't matter that she worked here, he had to have her. *Yes sir, Miss Eliza Monroe will be a dream come true.* He watched as she pushed the obese man out of the room. Grinning and chuckling to himself, he pushed his cart.

The rain continued through the week. A cold front stalled over the city and sat idle. It was expected to cause high tides and some minor coastal erosion. Janice looked out the window to the street. She wondered if the rain had washed away the stink of the neighborhood yet. Used to be kind of nice. When Lawrence was at work, Janice would sit on the front steps and bask in the sun. The lady next door, Linda, would come over and chat. Back then they called it gossiping. There always was plenty going on to provide some new juicy secret. Linda had moved to the West Coast with her husband. She had written once then stopped. Janice understood. The way things looked, she wouldn't want to look back either. The past was over; the future was ...

And the rain fell.

Janice had pressed a shirt for Simon to wear. Not the one he told her to, so she pulled the ironing board out again as he showered.

Eliza was all he could think about today. He

hadn't seen her, but perhaps she was off. Tonight would be heaven. Simon made reservations at the swanky restaurant in town. "Tie required" boasted their Yellow Pages advertisement. His only necktie was purchased for his father's funeral. He found the crumpled strip of cloth in a drawer and, after looking it over, decided she had better iron it also. He yelled out his door for her to come get it. Her footfalls on the steps shook the mirror slightly while he was trimming his nose hairs.

She gasped entering the room. He looked like Lawrence. Faking a smile, she took the tie and headed back downstairs.

With shaky hands, Simon attempted to tie the knot for the third time. He had figured it couldn't be too difficult, but he always ended with a deformed mess around his neck.

"Ma!" He trailed her to the kitchen.

Holding the ironed tie, Janice turned him to look at her and gripped both ends of the fabric. "The rabbit hops over the log. The rabbit crawls under the log. The rabbit runs around the log. The rabbit dives through the rabbit hole at the top end of the log." Her hands worked as she spoke and patted down a perfect knot.

Simon gave her a boyish grin and blushed. "Thanks," he snickered.

A crack of lightning made them both jump a bit as the power went out. Janice felt her way into the darkness and returned with a flashlight. She was careful to keep the beam aimed to the floor until she was able to strike a match to a hurricane lamp. Replacing the globe and adjusting the wick, it filled the room with a warm glow.

"I haven't seen one of those lit in years," Simon observed. "I remember Dad didn't care for the stench they left in the room." He sniffed the air and angled his head as if in thought. "Ya know, he was right. Turn that thing off when I leave. I don't want the house stinking when I get back." Simon glared at her and raised an eyebrow, curving the edges of his lips in a forced smile. "Don't wait up."

Janice watched him walk out the door. Her hands shook uncontrollably.

Jake sat out in front of Eliza's home, keeping an eye on the lights and the windows of surrounding homes. Some nosy bitch could mess everything up. In the dark he jogged to her door. He considered turning back. Too close to home, too dangerous. She took several minutes to open the door. He stood with his back to her, then spun and lashed out. The hypodermic needle pierced her neck just above the collar. Shit, she had her purse in her hand, Jake noticed. She was expecting someone. He took her by the arm and walked her to the car. The rain was falling hard now. She collapsed onto the passenger seat as headlights turned the corner. Jake averted his face from the car as it drove slowly past, but the dome light had been on. Even in this downpour, he could smell her perfume. He couldn't wait to know her body, take his time. She was gonna be a masterpiece. As he climbed into the driver's seat, he stroked back his hair. Looking over at her, he felt his groin coming to life. Yeah, it was gonna be one hell of a night.

Simon beat on his steering wheel. He watched a man helping Eliza into his car in the rain. Saw her sitting, waiting to be driven away. The plastic trim of the wheel cracked in the center and fell to his lap. She couldn't have possibly forgotten, could she? Some other piece of shit just gonna step in and take his date? Simon screamed out in rage within the confines of the automobile. The rain pounded the vehicle. He drove to the end of the road and turned around in a cul-de-sac. The car was gone when he got back. Eliza was gone ...

Fucking bitch.

Bellowing in a fit of rage, Simon crashed through the door of his darkened house and rushed to his room. Janice cowered in her bed. It had been a long time since she was able to comfort him. Best to stay out of his way. He kicked his door open and continued his rampage. The lady must have done something really awful. Janice knew that she was the one who would pay for it though. Then she could hear him in the darkened living room kicking the furniture and throwing things against walls. Her heart dropped when she thought of her valentine being smashed. She hopped out of bed and raced down the stairs.

Electric was restored to grid 87 at 9:25 pm. Lightning strike, Breakers. A man notated in his logbook before throwing it on the dashboard and driving the bucket truck away from a repaired transformer. The wet roads glowed from streetlights. He was in a hurry to get back to his daughter's wedding rehearsal dinner. There was gonna be hell to pay later from his wife

The room was destroyed. The lights came on as she reached the foot of the stairs. Simon had worked his way into the kitchen, and it sounded like he was using the refrigerator as a practice dummy. The floor would shake on its foundation as he hit the appliance. That didn't matter to Janice. The frame of the small valentine lay on the floor broken. The pink hearts ripped up in the broken glass.

"NO!" Janice screamed.

The pummeling on the refrigerator stopped.

"YOU HAD NO RIGHT! You had no right." Her voice trailed off to a whisper. How she hated Lawrence. How she hated her father. How she hated men. Her last hope destroyed. She tried to piece the mutilated valentine on the floor back together. The pink paper turned dark with the drops of her tears. Ruined.

She looked up at Simon, his shirt torn, but there was no regret on his face, just anger. Janice grabbed the coffee table leg.

"Why, Simon, why?" She tried to see anything but his own self-pity but there was nothing. "When I found out I was pregnant with you from that … man," she felt her stomach churning, " I was ready to throw myself off the piers. But all I could think was this child was an innocent. He's not a monster like his father. I was wrong."

Simon studied his mother's face. *Doesn't this silly bitch understand what pain I'm in? What the fuck's her problem compared to mine?* "You don't talk about Dad that way! He always made sure you had food, and a place to sleep. All you had to do was keep it clean and spread your legs for him once in a while. SO DON'T YOU DARE TALK ABOUT MY FATHER!" He raised his fist. The coffee table leg connected with his jaw.

Turning his head back, he spat out a few teeth. Simon felt his mouth fill with blood. She swung again, but he caught it in his hand.

"Ungrateful bitch, all I ever tried to do is fill the space in your life since Dad died." He drooled blood out the corners of his mouth as he spoke. "I guess it wasn't enough, huh?" Simon snatched the leg from her grasp.

He swung … and again.

Eyes lowered, he dropped the leg. And went into the downstairs bathroom.

Janice crawled to the kitchen. The floor was covered with broken dishes, and as she crept forward they dug into her skin. The phone lay on the floor with the rhythmic tones of being off the hook. She pressed 911. It was answered immediately. Her face was too broken to speak. Janice choked and drowned in her own blood. The emergency operator called out louder.

Simon held a towel to his mouth as he ascended the stairs to his room. The sounds of the city seemed so near. Sirens wailed in the distance. He sat on his bed. Looking up into his window, he could see that guy had a new date tonight.

Jake stood over Eliza. She was beginning to stir. Using his knife, he slowly cut the clothing off her. Taking his time, until she lay naked on the floor. He marveled at her body, so firm and full. The finest he'd ever had. He looked through the window and saw Simon, then waved to him. "Wanna watch, you sick fuck?" Jake whispered.

Simon's heart pounded wildly. *It was Eliza! That asshole had Eliza!* He screamed, "You're fucking dead if you touch her, DEAD!" The man just smiled and waved again. Simon could hear beating on his door. He was paralyzed to the spot.

Jake grabbed the back of her head and, while Simon watched, sliced open her throat. Blood covered his legs as he pumped his member into her new orifice. Smiling at the man. He was yelling something. Didn't matter. Holding her head, he reached orgasm quickly.

Simon yelled out as the police broke into his room.

"Let the girl go!" the officer ordered.

Simon looked down and saw Eliza's body at his feet. Her head in his hands.

He looked at the mirror on the wall.

Jake was laughing.